COURT HASLETT is the author of the *Sleeper Hayes* crime series set in San Francisco's Tenderloin neighborhood. A San Francisco and Bay Area resident for over 20 years, his work has been shortlisted for the Faulkner-Wisdom Award.

A 280 STEPS PAPERBACK

Tenderloin is a work of fiction. The characters are entirely imaginetive creations of the author, and any resemblance between these fictional characters, and actual persons, living or dead, is purely coincidental.

First published as an eBook November 2013 by The Rogue Reader

This paperback edition first published in 2017

ISBN 978-82-9332-676-2

Visit us at www.280steps.com

A SLEEPER HAYES NOVEL

TENDERLOIN

COURT HASLETT

280
STEPS

For Matt

The less reasonable a cult is, the more men seek to establish it by force.

Jean-Jacques Rousseau

There is in all men a demand for the superlative, so much so that the poor devil who has no other way of reaching it attains it by getting drunk.

Oliver Wendell Holmes, Jr.

PROLOGUE

On November 18th, 1978, 918 members of Jim Jones's Peoples Temple died in the jungles of Guyana from drinking poisoned Flavor-Aid. Some drank willingly, others were forced at gunpoint. None of the 276 children were given a choice in the matter.

Though the massacre occurred over 4,000 miles from Northern California, San Francisco is where the seeds of this tragedy were planted and where Jim Jones was allowed to grow into the twisted, deadly monster he became.

Ultimately, the blame for the Jonestown Massacre rests with Jones, his henchmen, and the misguided souls who dedicated their lives to him. But the city of San Francisco also deserves blame. Blame for enabling him, for feeding his megalomania, and for ignoring the insurmountable evidence that the Temple had become something sinister, something capable of committing reprehensible acts on its members, including murder.

1978

I

Friday, August 18th, 10 p.m.

"Read 'em and weep. Three Queens."

"Stifle the play-by-play, would ya?" I said.

"Take it easy, Sleeper. He was just joking," Dom said, defending the newbie at our weekly game.

"First, a joke implies laughter," I said. "Second, I know the rules of poker. I don't need Howard Cosell over there to explain them to me."

"Hey, I thought this was a friendly game," Three Queens chirped.

"Need a friend? Buy a ham radio."

"Hey, screw you," he said, and any remnants of affability left the room. Good. I could now concentrate, guilt-free, on busting this chump.

It only took a few hands to complete this task, once again proving the old adage about a fool and his money. I was sitting on a pair of eights when he opened the betting at twenty-five dollars. Pretty aggressive for a guy down to his last fifty. I sensed desperation and called him. Dom, Johnny, Clyde, and Yuri sensed it also and folded, allowing me to do their dirty work. It was the type of job I'd grown accustomed to, both at the poker table and in the rest of my life.

Three Queens asked for one card and I waited for the tell. *The pause.* When a player asks for one card, he either has two pair or he's gunning for a straight or flush. If he has two pair, then he'll pick up the card effortlessly, because it's already a decent hand.

But if the player takes his time before looking, if he pauses, then he needs the card to make his hand. It's do or die. Like any do-or-die situation, people slow down and focus, as if they can will the outcome to their favor. Whether that intense concentration is aimed at a judge handing down a sentence, a mad man pointing a gun at you, or in this case, a card to make your inside straight, it's easy to spot and rarely a winning strategy.

Three Queens paused for what in reality was two seconds. In poker time, it was an eternity. He was gunning for the straight, most likely an inside one at that.

"I'm going big or going home," he said, sliding his remaining chips into the middle of the table.

"More insightful commentary," I replied, matching his bet. I laid my hand down first. Bad form, I know, but I couldn't help myself. He'd been grating on me all night and I wanted him to know that I'd called his bluff with nothing.

He placed his cards on the table, face down, stood up, and slid on his jacket. He started to say something to me, then, deciding against it, settled on, "Thanks for the game, fellas."

His graciousness almost made me feel bad. I was already carrying around enough regret, mostly about my ex-wife, Maggie, but also about the myriad decisions that had led me from a prominent role in the hippie movement to a prominent role on Tenderloin's skid row in a few short years. I wasn't about to waste any remorse on this all-too-chatty poker hack.

After the door closed, Johnny scolded me. "Sleeper, do you have to be like that to every new guy who sits down? That's easy money you keep scaring off."

"Somebody has to teach the world proper etiquette," I replied.

"Who are you, Miss Fucking Manners?" Clyde said.

"That's Mr. Manners to you. All of you knew I had rags. He should have known it, too."

"Rags?" Yuri asked.

"Yeah, rags."

"Rags?" he repeated.

"Crap cards, you dumb Commie. How come that computer you have for a brain can't process English?"

"Process English?"

"Ah, forget it," I said, never knowing for sure when Yuri was putting me on. "Deal the cards," I said to Niko, who ran the nightly games above the Acropolis Café for his cousin and owner, Dmitri.

We played another two hours of blissful, commentary-free poker. Even after flipping Niko his standard ten percent, and laying down a bet on the Red Sox with Dmitri on the way out, I left the game sixty dollars richer, more than enough to cover my expenses for the next week or two.

I walked down to the Triangle to celebrate with Lori, my latest bartender-girlfriend. Starting with my ex-wife, Maggie, I'd established a distinct pattern of dating women who worked behind the bar. Not all that surprising, given that bars were where I spent the bulk of my free time. It also helped that compared to the other drunks and crazies in the Tenderloin, I was a steal. Attractiveness is often determined by the alternatives around you. It had taken awhile, but I'd found a level of competition I could dominate. Finally, though I would never fully admit it to myself, I think I was trying to recreate that spark between Maggie and myself from six years ago, when we first met at Muriel's Trophy Room on Haight Street.

The Tipsy Triangle, the Square Chair, and the Round Table were three joints on Leavenworth Street that straddled the line between bar and brothel. For a cut of the take, the owners allowed pros to pick up johns in their establishments. In return, the women received a warm, safe place to ply their trade.

Assuming you were a known quantity, these bars were also the safest places to drink in the Tenderloin, or the T.L. as we residents called it. They were the Tenderloin equivalent of a private country club, no admittance unless someone vouches for you. Unlike the Square and the Circle, which took the country club comparison one-step further by banning minorities, the Triangle was still an equal opportunity purveyor of sex.

I met Lori one night looking for my buddy Lyle. Lyle had developed an expensive addiction to Lollipop, a big leggy blonde who worked out of the Triangle and knew exactly how many licks it took to get to the center. Lyle was delayed by a pool game at Hollywood Billiards, so I passed the time with Lori. We hit it off after I declined to join a conversation with another couple by saying, "Three's company."

Lori caught my attention when she responded with the appropriate Peaches and Herb line, "but four's a traffic jam."

Only a bartender forced to listen to the jukebox all day or a pop music obsessive like myself, would have made that connection. Two months later, our quasi-relationship was clicking along at a decent tempo.

Lori, who overcame her mousy-brown hair with a sly smile, a playful spark in her green eyes, and the legs of a long jumper, reached for the Johnnie Red when I walked in after the poker game with Three Queens.

"Make it Black tonight, baby," I said.

"Somebody won a few pots."

"Don't look so surprised."

"The only surprising thing you could do is leave a big tip," she said, handing me my drink with a wink and a kiss.

Lori was a trailblazer for women's rights at the Triangle. Like all the other bartenders there, she was an ex-con. Unlike all the others, she was a she. The first woman Frank hired to work behind the bar. That was the extent of women's lib in the T.L. in 1978.

I took a sip and surveyed the room. The Triangle, like the entire T.L., had caught me in its net when I was falling, and like thousands of others who landed safely here, I was now unable or unwilling to wriggle free of its web. That might sound crazy to an outsider, but the Tenderloin, like many skid rows, was teeming with life. The fact that it drew its vitality from the seedy side of the street was just an added bonus for me.

I didn't even have to look outside the Triangle to witness the Tenderloin's spark that night. The Triangle was hopping. At the small back tables, a couple of johns were negotiating deals with women. If you didn't know better you'd think they were lovestruck teenagers on a first date. Next to me at the bar, Desma and Bunny were sipping vodka tonics, waiting for prospective johns.

At the other end of the bar was another regular, George Urbancyck, the president of Local 261, the most powerful union in the city. George was a throwback to the old days when union leaders weren't lawyers with business degrees, but scrappers with larger-than-life personalities. He wore pinstripes with matching hats, weaved a Shakespeare quotation into every conversation—often with a choice curse word artfully inserted—and ate five nights a week at the House of Prime Rib. He had a blurb for every reporter and advice for every politician seeking Local 261's support.

George was a regular customer of Cindy's. She wasn't his girlfriend, because he did still have to pay, but everyone knew that George took precedence over her other dates. We raised our glasses to one another across the bar, and I polished off my drink.

"See you later?" I asked Lori.

"Is that an invitation?"

"If you want it to be."

"How romantic. Why can't you be more like George?" Lori asked. "He dotes on Cindy."

"Not so much tonight," I said.

George and Cindy were in the middle of a rare argument that was starting to make the rest of the patrons uncomfortable. Not surprisingly, it was about the Peoples Temple. Cindy was an ex-member who was now one if its most vociferous opponents. I couldn't imagine what the argument could be about. By this point, we'd all heard Cindy's rants hundreds of times. Nevertheless, something about the Temple was under both of their skins.

"Still," she said, batting her eyes.

"Okay, how about this: 'When that old sweet tooth comes around,'" I quoted our newest favorite Peaches and Herb song.

"'No use searching all over town,'" she followed.

"'I can whip up some goodies tonight.'"

"'You and I and the stereo light,'" she ended, and picked up my empty glass. "Fine, I'll be there."

"You're just like the song," I said. "'Easy as Pie.'"

2

A conspicuously well-dressed man stood at attention on the doorstep of my apartment building, welcoming me home.

"Mr. Hayes?" he asked.

"Never heard of him." I brushed past the stranger and stuck my key in the lock.

He grabbed the door handle. "Mr. Hayes, please come with me. I really don't have to ask." He flashed his badge and motioned toward an idling Ford LTD.

"I have two rules in life," I said. "Never bet the Don't Pass Line in craps and never get in a car with an FBI agent. Mind telling me what this is about?"

"It's about saving your life," he replied.

"Leave the religion game to the Pope."

"We have evidence of a plot against your life. Do you want to come with me or not?"

If I had to compromise one of my rules, I was glad it was this one. Even for a non-believer like myself, betting on someone to crap out on the Don't Pass Line was a little too close to the bad karma line.

"Let's go," I agreed.

We didn't have much time to get to know one another on the short drive to the FBI's office. We zipped down Hyde a few blocks and turned west onto Golden Gate, ignoring the one-way signs heading east. After a screeching U-turn, we parked in front of the Federal Building. My chaperone escorted me into an empty conference room on the 12th floor.

"Stay here. My boss will be in to see you soon."

Ten minutes later, an older, more ragged version of the agent who escorted me here entered the room. A female assistant wheeled in a tape deck the size of a suitcase, plugged the bulky contraption into an electrical socket, and exited.

"Thanks for coming in, Mr. Hayes," he began. "I'm Ray Maguire."

I knew his name. He was the director of the San Francisco Division of the FBI, a post that had become prominent during the sixties and had remained high profile since, as they and the CIA were still seemingly investigating everyone and everything in San Francisco. The bloated bags under Maguire's eyes and his midnight coffee were evidence of his extensive workload.

"Sleeper," I said.

"Right, I forgot. Sleeper."

"If this is Candid Camera you can tell Al to come out now."

"I'm afraid it's not a joke, so I'll get right to it. You know who Captain Walt Stezak is?" he asked.

"Everyone in the T.L. knows that cocksucker." Stezak was the police captain who ran the Tenderloin like his own banana republic.

"Well, he seems to have a keen dislike of you."

Stezak and I had butted heads last year over the suicide

13

of a friend's brother. He even worked me over with that stick he's always twirling around, like the drum major of a bent cop parade.

"I dislike most people," I replied. "That's not a Federal offense, is it?" Authority figures always brought out the best in me.

"No, but killing someone is, and that's what Stezak has planned for you," Maguire replied.

"Hmm."

"Pretty blasé response."

"Pretty blasé world."

"Well, maybe this will liven it up for you." He leaned over and pressed play on the tape recorder. "The first guy talking is his right-hand man, Sergeant Porto."

"Saw that Sleeper prick at the Acropolis laying some bets the other day. You want me to pick him up?"

"No. I got something else planned for that one. Won't require a jail cell either."

Maguire stopped the tape. "You have any idea why he wants you out of the picture?" he asked.

"No, but I bet you do."

"Actually, we don't. We were hoping you could enlighten us."

"Wait a minute. You brought me in here to ask why someone wants to kill me, someone I didn't even know wanted to kill me before you brought me in? Makes me dizzy thinking about it," I said.

"What we were hoping was that if you helped us, maybe we could help keep you alive. We've been investigating Stezak

14

for awhile, but we can't get any solid evidence against him."

"You think I can give you solid evidence against Stezak?"

"That was the hope. He must have some reason to want you dead. Maybe you saw him doing something he shouldn't have been doing?"

"Everyone in the T.L. has seen Stezak doing something he shouldn't be doing," I said.

"Everyone has a story, but nobody will go on record because they're scared shitless of him. The one person we have him threatening on tape is you. You sure you don't know anything that could help us out?"

He was right. I did have something on Stezak, but I couldn't help him. Anything I offered Maguire would jeopardize my ex-wife and I wasn't about to do that again. Maggie had been unjustly imprisoned last year, and in order to get her out, I had to sit on evidence that could implicate a whole host of bad guys, including Stezak. Part of the deal I made was that if I ever unsat on what I knew, Maggie would be the first to feel the fallout.

"Nothing like that," I lied. "I popped off one night at Donny D's and he gave me a tune-up. I didn't go down without a fight. I managed to bust his lip with a haymaker. Maybe his pride is still hurt from that. I don't know."

"You punched Stezak in the face and lived to tell about it?" Maguire asked.

"I'm here, aren't I?"

"Hmm."

"Pretty blasé response."

"Pretty blasé world."

I had that one coming.

3

Saturday, August 19th, 1:30 a.m.

I stepped out into the frigid nighttime air. Wired by my meeting with Maguire, I took the long way home. I noticed a dim light glowing from the back of Newman's Gym. I gave the door a few hard pounds in hopes of retrieving my bible—the racing form—that I'd forgotten there earlier in the day.

It wasn't the owner, Billy Newman, who answered the door. It was Alfredo Flores, the promising young professional who trained there. When Alfredo was sixteen, Billy had given him a key to the place. Alfredo had lived there ever since, training during the day and sleeping in the storage room at night. From the looks of Alfredo now, sweaty and out of breath, he'd taken his training for his upcoming fight to another level.

"Hey, Sleeper," he greeted me in his upbeat manner.

"Hey, Alfredo. Billy around?"

"Nah. He's long gone."

"Working overtime for the Martinez fight, huh?" I asked. "You really worried about him?"

"Come on, man. What do you think?"

"How's your weight?"

"One-fifty. Three pounds over. It won't be a problem."

"Alright," I said, faking concern. "You sparring tomorrow?"

"Noon sharp. You coming?"

"Wouldn't miss it. Hey, I left my racing form here today. Mind if I grab it?" I asked, stepping past him.

"Hey, uh, before you go in..."

I saw Billy's office light on from down the hall. "I thought you said Billy wasn't here," I shouted over my shoulder.

"Sleeper!" Alfredo yelled back as I opened and shut the office door in the time it takes to snap a photo. What developed in my mind was a naked woman covering up and shrieking. It took another moment to realize the woman in the photo was Nancy Sherman, co-owner of the laundromat across the street. The other owner was her husband, Fred.

"I tried to warn you," Alfredo said, giggling.

"And here I thought you were working out."

"Hey, don't tell Ricky, man. I'm supposed to be abstaining for the fight." Ricky was Alfredo's overzealous brother and trainer who guarded over Alfredo like the valuable commodity he was.

"I'm no fink."

"Thanks, Sleeper," he said. "I know you're not."

My racing form was right where I left it, on the upper left row of the bleachers.

"Stay out of trouble," I said to Alfredo on my way out.

"I should say the same to you."

17

4

Saturday, August 19ᵗʰ, 2 a.m.

I returned to the Crescent, the apartment building I managed for my hippie friend, Jake, who'd inherited it from his slumlord father. Jake, having no interest in running a flophouse in the T.L., paid me a small stipend to live in its tiny, first floor studio and take care of the building. So long as the place didn't blow up or bankrupt him, Jake left me pretty much alone. Those were the precise terms I'd tried unsuccessfully to negotiate with the rest of the world: Stay out of my way and I'll stay out of yours. Why I hadn't found other takers for such a seemingly simple deal was one of the great disappointments of my life.

I bypassed my room and walked up a flight of stairs to smoke some weed and listen to music with Nelson, my crippled, dope-smoking guru of a best friend. His door was ajar. If this were 6 p.m., the beginning of his lone dope-selling hour of the day, then the open door wouldn't have caught my eye.

I tapped on the doorframe, in case he had made a rare exception to his rigid business hour. I poked my head into

18

the room.

"Nelson?" I called out.

"Down here, Sleeper," he whispered. I looked down and saw a cane and a pair of hush puppies sticking out from behind his couch.

I hustled over and helped him off the floor. His cardigan and cords were stained with blood from his nose. His glasses were missing, his left eye was pink and puffy, and his short afro was flattened on one side.

"You okay?" I asked. "What happened?"

"Couple a punks rolled me. I should have never let them up after hours. They took my weed and my money. Knocked me out for a little bit, too. You see my glasses anywhere?"

I scanned the room without any luck. I did see something else missing, though, something much more important than Nelson's glasses: his record collection.

"Oh, man," I muttered and sat down next to him. "You see what else they took?"

He followed my gaze to where his records used to be. "Oh, no," he said, struggling to his feet, before giving up midway and falling back onto the couch.

Nelson's record collection wasn't any old collection. His was a collector's collection. Nelson had acquired his records over three decades, with impeccable curating skills, every album selected with the utmost care and appreciation. He owned a cross-section of rare, live, and limited-edition albums from every genre. It was his life's achievement. I doubted the punks who robbed him even knew what they had stumbled upon. They had intended to simply rip off a hobbled drug dealer. The records were an unexpected bonus. Little did they know those records were worth ten times whatever they stole in weed.

"What am I gonna do without my music, Sleeper?"

"I don't know, buddy," I said. "I don't know."

5

Saturday, August 19th, 10 a.m.

I awoke the next morning upright on Nelson's couch. Nelson was slouched over on the opposite arm, his pink eye purpling. By noon, it would be blackened.

I worried about my friend. Those records had been Nelson's constant companions ever since a bus crushed his feet as a teenager on the south side of Chicago, essentially confining him to his couch. They were Nelson's life, his memories, his soul.

Nelson was always my sounding board when life became overwhelming. Years of nearly constant smoking had slowed and slurred his speech. Some people mistook this for a slowness of the mind. It's true that Nelson's logic wasn't always straightforward, nor his delivery articulate, but his take on any topic was always unexpected and enlightening.

I knew his counsel wasn't for everyone, though. If you're the conventional type, then his steadfast belief in sterilizing the very rich and the very poor wouldn't spin your top. Nor would you believe his claim that he and Yuri wrote the outline for the SALT treaty. But if you were looking for weed, a fresh opinion, and a laugh, like I always seemed to be, then Nelson was your guy. I considered him my personal, stoned, black Buddha.

I searched Nelson's apartment and found his broken glasses on the floor by the makeshift kitchen. I took them upstairs to Lady Ellinger, our resident den mother, who Scotch-taped them together the best she could. I placed them back on Nelson's coffee table and eased myself out of his room.

Under my apartment door was a note from Lori. "When is an invite not an invite? When it comes from Sleeper Hayes. Thanks for nothing." Shit. In the hubbub of the FBI visit and Nelson's attack, I'd forgotten she was meeting me here after work.

Oh, well, I shrugged. Though this quirky, tough, ex-con bartender encapsulated everything I loved about the T.L., namely proof that diamonds in the rough do exist, I'd carefully designed my life so as not to have to take anything seriously, even diamonds. Lori had been apprised of this set-up early and often, which is why I chose not to dwell on the fact that she, like most people, heard what she wanted to hear, and not what was said.

I needed a quick shower and breakfast before going down to Newman's to watch Alfredo spar. I splurged on Italian sausage, hash browns, and eggs over easy at Sontiya's Café. At $2 a plate, it wasn't the cheapest breakfast in the T.L., but when your morning needed a kick-start for whatever reason, whether it's being hung over, remembering that a psychopath with a uniform wants you dead, or in my case, both, it was money well spent.

I arrived at Newman's at eleven, an hour before it opened

to the public. Billy Newman took over the gym, a converted dining room in the Cadillac Hotel, back in 1948. It'd been a Tenderloin cornerstone ever since. Everyone from a young Cassius Clay to Miles Davis to George Foreman had worked out at Newman's, as well as any San Francisco amateur worth his salt. Nobody paid any attention to the 'Members Only' sign. Billy allowed anyone in so long as they behaved, and even the troublemakers got multiple warnings.

He granted me an even longer leash than most because Billy loved horseracing almost as much as he loved a perfectly executed combination. We spent many mornings handicapping the local races at Golden Gate Fields and Bay Meadows before the gym opened. Billy has a great instinct for the horses. His picks were always solid overlays that ran much better than the odds indicated they would. Unfortunately, they also came up a head short most of the time. This result was problematic only because Billy refused to bet his horses to place, even though they often would have paid double digits. Place bets were beneath him. Lacking any semblance of pride, I'd never had that problem.

This difference in our gambling styles also reflected the varying reasons Billy and I bet the horses in the first place. Billy loved the underdog. He wanted to pick out a worthy long shot and ride him to glory.

What I wanted from gambling was a place where logic and common sense prevailed. A place where the outcome wasn't rigged against you. A place that required using hunches and deductive reasoning, skepticism and leaps of faith, all in equal parts. Yes, I'm aware of the irony in believing that the racetrack, a notoriously shady setting, was fairer than everyday life. That irony doesn't make it any less true.

The long entry hall was lined with fight posters from past and present. Locals like Vinnie Hines and Kerry Mullins received equal billing with legends like Liston and Frazier. In a few years, I thought to myself, Alfredo's poster would be the most prized of all.

I passed the telephone booth and Billy's office, where Billy and Ricky, Alfredo's brother, were huddled up in a strategy session. I waved my form at Billy and took a seat on the top row of bleachers beside the ring. Alfredo was skipping rope across the room next to one of the formal columns, a reminder of the room's culinary pedigree. He saw my reflection in the mirror and flashed a smile.

Alfredo's opponent in his next bout was Hector Martinez, a scrappy, quick journeyman. Hector was managed by Pete Castillo, an integral part of the local boxing scene. Pete was integral not because he produced any great fighters, but because he managed all the tomato cans in town, offering them up as red meat to the real boxers. Pete missed his true calling as an actor, though. After every beating one of his fighters took—and we were well into the hundreds by now—Pete would feign the same shock and indignation at the decision. Needless to say, Hector Martinez was not going to lay a glove on Alfredo.

Alfredo's sparring partners straggled in and began taping their hands, stretching, and shadow boxing. Today's opponents looked like all the others he'd been sparring with lately, featherweights. These speed bugs were Ricky's way of preparing Alfredo, a welterweight, for the fleet-footed Martinez.

As Alfredo dismantled his first opponent, I thought about last night's visit with the FBI. How worried should I be about

Stezak's not-so-veiled threat? I couldn't completely brush it off. Stezak was a certifiable psycho who'd brutalized the neighborhood for almost two decades.

Yet the more I thought about it, the less concerned I was. Even if Stezak had lost a little face in our standoff last year, he had to have bigger fish to fry than me, didn't he? And who knows when that tape was recorded? It could have been last year, right after the incident between us, when emotions were still running hot. Nah, he was onto his next two-bit scam by now.

Billy, all 130 pounds of him, joined me on the bleachers halfway through Alfredo's second sparring partner. Billy wore his trademark gray, ratty sweats and a porkpie hat that covered his short, curly white hair.

"Anything jumping out at you?" he asked, nodding to the racing form.

"Nah. Pretty chalky."

"Damn chalk. Nobody likes the favorites but housewives and insurance salesmen."

"I like one favorite," I replied.

"Who's that?"

I nodded to Alfredo.

"About time we got one," Billy agreed.

"He as good as I think?" I asked.

"Best I've seen. No weaknesses in the ring."

"How about outside it?"

"The usual," Billy replied.

"Which is?"

"You want the short or long version?"

"Short, of course," I answered.

"A woman."

"And the long?"

"Women."

"My kind of problem."

Billy chuckled. "Yeah, well Alfredo's stamina in that department knows no bounds. You see that scratch on his neck? Ricky says some crazy broad smashed an alarm clock on him."

"Why, she find out about another woman?"

"No. She wanted an hour of sleep and Alfredo wanted another hour of her."

"Another hour? Shit, I have to round up to get to 30 minutes."

"Boxing and women, both young men's games," Billy said.

On cue, Don Stewart, another trainer at Newman's, walked in and pulled my sleeve. "Hey Sleeper, some girl is looking for you out front."

"Good one, Don."

"I'm serious. I told her to come back when we're open, but she insisted I track you down."

"Five-foot-eight, light brown hair?" I asked.

"That's the one."

"Christ. You stand a girl up once and it's like Watergate all over again."

I clambered down the bleachers and down the hall. Lori was pacing outside, crying.

"I'm sorry I forgot about last night," I began. "I had the worst night—"

"Cindy's dead."

6

Saturday, August 19th, 12 p.m.

Lori gave me the details on the walk back to the Triangle. "She was found strangled in her apartment this morning."

"Strangled?" I asked.

"Oh, God." Lori started crying again.

"Who did she leave the bar with last night?"

"George."

Walking back to the Triangle in silence, I remembered their lovers' quarrel at the bar, which was all it seemed like at the time, a lovers' quarrel.

George and I went back ten years at least, to when I was active in the peace movement. Though not on the same page culturally, hippies and unions were often political allies. George was forced to meet with us more than I'm sure he'd wanted. I always liked his colorful personality and I think he got a kick out of me, too. I found it hard to swallow that George would kill Cindy, particularly over some argument about the Reverend Jim Jones.

A couple of the girls, Bunny and Desma, were already at the Triangle, along with Frank, the owner, Vic, the bartender, and Simon, Cindy's pimp. The girls looked sad, Vic and Frank looked stunned, and Simon looked pissed off.

"Hey, Frank," I offered my hand. "What happened?"

"Simon went over to her place this morning for last night's take and found her dead."

"She was laying there all peaceful like," Simon added. "Even had a little gold angel sitting on her chest."

"A gold angel?" I repeated. "That's strange. Anyone seen George?"

"Not yet," Simon rumbled.

Simon was not someone you wanted on your bad side. He was in his mid-50s, Irish, with a nose like a silver dollar pancake and a body like a tank. He'd come up the hard way, working corners, sending girls behind dumpsters, and handling any problem johns himself. He had performed dental work, rhinoplasty, and other orthopedic services, free of charge, to anyone who so much as looked at his girls the wrong way. Who could blame him? This was the T.L., where a stern lecture doesn't persuade anyone.

Simon had forged his way to respectability, pimping girls like Cindy, who were not quite call girls, but not streetwalkers, either. His girls benefited from his reputation as well. They were neither threatened nor touched by their johns anymore, ever. Not Simon's girls. I had no doubt that he took this attack on Cindy as an attack on himself.

"You don't think George could have done this, do you? They were practically married," Lori said.

"Tell that to his real wife," Frank said.

"George is married?" Bunny asked.

"Thirty-five years."

"Wow. Who knew?"

"Everybody," Frank said.

"I still don't think he would do anything like that. You don't have to be married to be in love," Desma offered. There was nothing quite so absurd, or touching, as listening to hookers espouse on the power of love.

"I don't know nothing about love," Simon said. "All I know is he better have a good alibi."

"I don't think it was George, Simon," I said. "Besides, you sure you want to mess with George? He's got friends on both sides of the tracks."

"Sleeper, let me ask you something. If somebody stole from you, would you care whether the guy who did it was rich or poor, or whether he had friends or not? Or would you want your goddamn money back?"

"The money's not coming back, Simon."

"No shit, Sleeper. But I can't have anyone else thinking they can steal from me, can I?"

"This isn't some T.L. loser you're talking about rolling. The cops and the union will care if something happens to George."

"Let me worry about the cops."

"Vic, can I get a shot of Johnnie?" I asked.

As Vic poured me a double, I considered what I was about to offer Simon. This was how my troubles always began, by putting myself somewhere I didn't belong. I used to fight this invisible undertow that often dragged me into dangerous and morally murky waters. I'd even moved to the Tenderloin a few years ago to try and hide from it.

That didn't work, either. Last year I'd got caught in the strongest current I'd ever faced. I realized then that I could no longer avoid these situations, that they would always find me. Just like Billy would always bet on horses that lose by a head, I would always stick my nose into every lost cause.

I shot down the Johnnie in two swallows and girded myself. "Simon, don't do anything stupid yet." I said. "Maybe I can help."

"You? How the fuck can you help?" Simon asked.

"I know George a little bit. Let me see what I can find out."

Simon sized me up. "Alright. Let me know what you learn," he said, slapping a $100 bill on the bar. "Remember," he whispered, "I'm your first call."

Uh oh. When a pimp gives you money it can mean one of two things: you're either the john or you're turning the trick. Either way, somebody is getting screwed.

7

Wednesday, August 23rd, 6 p.m.

It had been almost a week since Cindy's murder and the Triangle was still in mourning. I suspected it would be for some time. Cindy was an essential element of the Triangle. Her sincere, limitless curiosity drew people to her, and her to them. She made everyone feel like her best friend. Cindy was both sweet and bawdy, reliable and spontaneous. Most surprising was how this Tenderloin hooker maintained an endearing naiveté about the world. I supposed it was that naiveté that initially drew her to the Temple, as well.

Nobody, apart from Simon, thought George killed her. Some of the girls were worried that the killer was a Jack-the-Ripper type, targeting prostitutes. Others thought the Zodiac killer had returned. I thought they were all flattering themselves in a delusional way: believing a psychotic killer is out to kill you is merely another sad form of solipsism.

I waited for Assistant D.A. Tom Hammersmith and his preposterously low voice to meet me at my new local, Donny D's on Mason Street, at the eastern edge of the Tenderloin. Donny's had replaced the Jug as my regular after I got into an argument with Kevin, the owner, about which was the best horse of all time. Kevin had sworn it was Man o' War, not Secretariat. A spirited argument ensued, resulting in Kevin requesting my departure from the Jug for an indefinite period of time.

I hate having these absurd arguments over and over. To avoid this problem in other areas of life, here are the correct answers to all remaining bar trivia: Secretariat, Jim Brown, Babe Ruth, Johnny Unitas, Jacqueline Smith, Louis Armstrong, the Stones, Sugar Ray Robinson, Gin, Scotch, Bill Russell, and of course, Mary Ann from Gilligan's Island.

Hammersmith smirked and shook his head as he sat down next to me at the bar. "This is trouble," he said.

"You don't even know why I called you," I said.

"Trouble doesn't follow you around. It's your North Star," he replied.

"What are you, a fucking astrologist?"

"Astronomist."

"Whatever. If I'm so much trouble, then why are you here?" I asked.

"Morbid curiosity." Hammersmith nodded to Donny, who started shaking a Manhattan. "Okay. I'll bite. What have you gotten yourself mixed up in now?"

"I'm not mixed up in anything," I said.

"Uh huh."

"It's a friend of mine," I said.

"Uh huh."

"Well, a friend of a friend."

"What's her name?"

"How do you know it's a woman?"

Hammersmith stared at me.

"Okay, so it's a woman," I said.

"Uh huh."

"Stop saying 'Uh huh,' you jackass, and listen. A friend of a friend was murdered last night. A working girl."

"How?"

"Strangled."

"Police have any leads yet?" he asked.

"That's why I'm here," I said. "She was last seen with George Urbancyck."

"*The* George Urbancyck?"

"You know another one?"

"Hmm. You know he's not that popular in the D.A.'s office right now?"

"Why's that?" I asked.

"This Justice Department investigation of him. We're helping them out."

George had been making the wrong kind of headlines recently. His first lieutenant, Buster Lemmer, was under indictment for misuse of funds—not a hard charge to prove, given Buster's penchant for passing out pocketfuls of union cash like it was candy. Buster wasn't their ultimate prize, though. Everyone suspected the Feds were using him as leverage to roll on George.

"How come you're helping the Feds out?" I asked.

"Because they asked. If I could help put George away for this, it might get me out of the doghouse at work. A doghouse you got me in, by the way."

"Oh, not this again," I said.

"Yes, this again. You screwed me on that Wethersby thing and you know it."

Hammersmith and I had come together, and then parted

ways, on the same situation that got me sideways with Stezak, as well as the Chinese Mafia, a Tenderloin smut peddler, and Hammersmith's personal nemesis, Bill Wethersby, an unscrupulous defense attorney and local political kingmaker. Hammersmith wasn't happy that I'd let Wethersby and the rest of the scumbags off the hook in exchange for my ex-wife's freedom.

"You would have done the same thing if you were in my position," I said, assuming Hammersmith had someone he cared for the way I cared for Maggie. Despite considering Hammersmith a friend, I was suddenly troubled by the fact that I had no idea if that was the case.

"Finally! At least you admit it," he said, and raised his arms in mock triumph.

"Is that all you wanted from me, an admission?"

"It's a start to the healing process," he said.

I clinked his glass with mine and took down the rest of my Johnnie. "Then let the healing begin," I said.

"Okay. Tell me more about the victim."

"Cindy Teague. I don't know much about her other than she was an ex-Peoples Temple member. Her sister still belongs, and Cindy's life work, other than hooking, was to get her out of Guyana."

"Bunch of freaks," Hammersmith said. "So why did George kill her?"

"I don't think he did. George had been seeing her for five years. He was as faithful to her as a married man can be."

"So why am I here?" Hammersmith asked.

"The woman's pimp thinks George did it and he doesn't have to follow official police protocol, if you know what I mean."

"Maybe the pimp is right," Hammersmith said.

"Maybe the pimp is an idiot who couldn't count to ten if he lost a finger."

"I still don't know what you want from me."

"If and when the investigation clears George, as I think it will, how about a heads-up? I'd like to stop the pimp from doing something stupid."

"That's it?" Hammersmith asked.

"That's it."

"Alright. I'll keep my ear to the ground for you. But you have to let me know if you dig up anything that implicates George."

"Deal. Oh, one more thing about the murder. They found a gold angel on top of her."

"A gold angel? You sure?"

"Yeah, why?" I asked.

"No reason."

Now I knew why Hammersmith refused to play cards with me. He was a horrible liar. "If you're gonna bullshit me, the least you can do is buy me a drink."

"Hey, Donny," he called. "Another round."

"Much better," I said.

"Excuse me," a working girl sitting next to us interrupted, "are you talking about that girl who got strangled?"

"Yes," I said.

"It's such a tragedy. I don't understand people who could do something like that. It's like they're a different species than the rest of us."

"I know what you mean," I said. "I feel the same way about people who put bumper stickers on their cars."

She looked at me like I was the biggest jerk on earth.

"How can you joke about a thing like this?"

I wasn't joking.

"I'm sorry," I said.

She picked up her Chardonnay and slid down to the end of the bar.

Donny walked over, chuckling. "I'd add people who like drum solos to that list," he said.

"How about people who like Fleet Week?" I asked.

Donny laughed so hard he coughed, then continued coughing until he bent over and spit blood into the garbage. He composed himself with a glass of water.

"What's going on with that cough, Donny?" I asked.

"Nothing good."

"No?"

"No," he said. "I got another one, people who honk their horns when they drive through a tunnel."

"Oh, that's good," I said.

The two of us could have gone on all night spouting nonsense, but I promised to check in on Lori at the Triangle.

As usual, I should have opted for the nonsense.

8

Wednesday, August 23rd, 9:30 p.m.

Lori wasn't in her usual spot behind the bar when I arrived at the Triangle. Vic saw my inquisitive look, held up a Johnnie Red bottle, and gave me a despondent shrug.

I paid for my drink and wondered about Lori's absence. A twinge of foreboding sounded somewhere in the back of my mind. Lori was a former addict who'd been straight for almost two years. Had she fallen off the wagon? *Don't go there*, I said to myself. *You feel a twinge of foreboding in everything*. Stop by her apartment and you'll see there's another, understandable reason for her absence.

Lori lived at the T.L.'s ground zero, Jones at Eddy, right across the street from where the infamous Mickey's Cigar Store and Soda Fountain was in the 1930's. Of course, Mickey's wasn't infamous for selling cigars and soda, but for the women upstairs. Tenderloin retailing hadn't changed much in the last fifty years. Steve's Pizza was busted last month for hiring hookers as waitresses, giving new meaning to the term "Daily Special."

Lori had lived in the T.L. for eight years, interrupted

by a two-year stint in Frontera State Prison. I would have awarded her the Congressional Medal of Honor instead of locking her up for what she'd done. A heroin addict at the time, Lori's dealer and his friends attempted to gang rape her during one of her bad spells. She defended herself by throwing hot wax on one, stabbing another, then setting fire to the apartment.

Lori's stint in the joint awakened her from her drug-induced stupor. Realizing she wasn't ready to succumb to her disease, Lori got clean in jail, and had been sober ever since, almost two years.

I knocked on her door for five minutes straight, knowing all the while that her clean streak was over. Finally, I heard rumbling noises, followed by the lock opening. She collapsed in my arms, smelling of cheap wine and vomit.

Good, I thought, *alcohol is better than drugs.*

"I can't believe Cindy's dead," she cried.

"I know. Lay back down. Take it easy."

"I went to clean out her room and I couldn't do it."

"It's okay. Let me take care of you," I said.

This wasn't good. Even though Cindy had been instrumental in keeping Lori clean the last couple of years, I didn't buy that Lori's fall off the wagon was all about Cindy's murder. I'd seen this behavior in countless addicts—find an excuse, even a valid one, to start using again: a woman left me, a parent died, the president was shot. Any reason to avoid admitting the overriding truth, that they loved being stoned more than they liked being sober. It's a sentiment I knew all too well.

I stripped off her vomit-stained sweater and jeans, threw them in the hamper, redressed her with a pair of sweats and a T-shirt, and tucked her in bed. I fetched her a glass of water and some aspirin, poured out the half-bottle of fortified wine next to her bed, and replaced it with a trashcan.

"You have the key to Cindy's?" I whispered. "I'll box up her things." No sense making Cindy's murder a double homicide by driving Lori back into addiction.

Lori gestured to the kitchen table. I picked up the keys and closed the door. When I was out in the hall that twinge of foreboding I felt when Lori hadn't shown for work was no longer a twinge. It was a tidal wave.

9

After procrastinating at Bay Meadows racetrack over the weekend—and missing *two* goddamn daily doubles by a combined neck—I wandered over to Cindy's place on Pine and Mason, square in the nether region known as Tender Nob, not quite the Tenderloin but not Nob Hill, either. Judging by her respectable, decent-sized, one-bedroom apartment, hooking either paid more than I thought, or George was subsidizing her lifestyle more than I realized.

Cindy had fashioned a nice little home for herself. It was girlish, in a Southern kind of way. Lavenders and pinks with lots of frills and patterns. Both rooms were clean and orderly, if a little overstuffed with photos, chotskies, pillows, and a few books. I liked all the keepsakes. It signaled the presence of a sentimental soul.

There was a pile of flattened boxes in the hallway and a half-full box in the living room, the one Lori must have been packing before she fell apart.

I started packing with what interested me most, Cindy's music. She had a dozen or so records next to the Hi-Fi, mostly

40

Country Western. Tammy Wynette, Conway Twitty, Loretta Lynn, and of course the mandatory copy of *Tapestry* that every woman I've ever known owned. She also had a copy of *Parsley, Sage, Rosemary and Thyme* by Simon and Garfunkel. I tried to calculate how much her records would fetch at The Record Exchange. It was a decent chunk of change.

I took down Cindy's ten or so books from the lone shelf over the couch. There were a couple of poetry anthologies, *To Kill a Mockingbird*, *I'm Okay, You're Okay*, and a King James Bible.

I stripped down the bed, then tackled the closet. The juxtaposition of her tawdry work clothes next to her plain old jeans and sweaters ripped at my heartstrings. "It goes on," I repeated my life's maxim, borrowed from Robert Frost, while suppressing the sadness welling inside me. Even after thirty-five years on the planet, those were still the only three words of wisdom that sounded, to my ear, like they had any ring of truth to them.

I powered through the clothes until I opened a box in the corner devoted to Jim Jones and The Peoples Temple. I wasn't surprised to find it; Jim Jones was Cindy's obsession. She'd left the Temple a few years ago and now spent all her time telling anyone who would listen how insane it was. At first those of us at the Triangle laughed it off, thinking it was the rantings of the type of troubled soul who'd join the Temple in the first place. But after an article appeared a year ago in *New West* magazine detailing some of the same abuses Cindy had told us about, we took notice. I closed the box and pushed it back where I found it.

Thinking about selling Cindy's albums back to The Record Exchange gave me an idea about Nelson's stolen collection. I checked the time. I still had ten minutes before Bill closed up shop.

I jogged straight to Turk Street and went right to the used section. First the V's. Yep, Velvet Underground's *1969: The Velvet Underground Live*. Rare, but not impossible to find. Next, the M's. There it was. Willie Mitchell's *Ooh Baby, You Turn Me On,* and not the more famously titled *Soul Serenade*. Then, to the L's. That was the clincher. Nick Lowe's British debut, *Jesus of Cool*, and not the U.S. release *Pure Pop for Now People*. The chances that Bill had one of these LP's was slim, but all three? Damn near impossible. Somebody had sold him Nelson's stolen collection. I took the albums to the counter.

"What's happening, Sleeper? I thought you were a library guy," Bill asked, referring to my method of procuring music.

"I am. Can't beat the prices. When did these come in?"

"Yesterday. Hot stuff, huh?"

"Very hot, Bill." I gave him a look.

"What are you talking about?"

"Who brought these in here?" I asked.

"Some girl, young. Said they were her mom's."

"You believed her?"

"Why wouldn't I?"

"Because they're Nelson's," I said.

"Nelson's?"

"Yeah. He got robbed a couple of nights ago. They took his entire collection."

"Oh, man. What a drag. I guess I should have known by all the Mingus. Man, oh man. I paid two thousand for this stuff."

"Two thousand? That's serious money."

"It's a serious collection. I could clear four grand on it, easy. I knew it was too good to be true." He stared at the ceiling, looking for counsel. "What do you want me to do?"

"You got a list of the whole collection?" I asked.

"Of course." He pulled out the drawer and handed over his ledger with every album and the prices paid for each.

"Can you put these aside until Nelson raises the money?" I pleaded.

"How's Nelson gonna come up with that kind of scratch?"

"Can you set them aside or not?"

"Damn it, Sleeper. I didn't know they were stolen," he argued.

"I know. Can you put them aside?"

He tapped his fingers on the counter. "Two months. Three tops. Then they're back on the floor. I gotta pay rent. Fair?"

"Under the circumstances, yeah," I said, unnecessarily qualifying my approval. A lifelong T.L. resident, Bill knew all about the circumstances of our world.

10

Monday, August 28th, 6:30 p.m.

Returning home to give Nelson the good news, I spotted a brown Jaguar parked in front of my building. Brown Jags being as rare in the Tenderloin as World Series games at Wrigley Field, there was no mistaking its owner.

I opened the passenger door and sat down.

"Mr. Wethersby."

"Mr. Hayes." He looked sharp, as usual, in a brown double-breasted suit, horn-rimmed glasses, and thick, groomed, silver hair.

"You wanna take this conversation to the Jug? I do owe you a snort, after all."

"I'm fine right here," he replied.

"So whatsup, Bill?"

He looked relieved to get down to brass tacks. "You see this?" He handed me a copy of *The Chronicle,* folded over to display the headline, "The Jonestown Gun Running Operation."

I scanned the first few paragraphs and got the gist: The ATF was investigating gun smuggling by the Peoples Temple from San Francisco to Guyana. *Another article for Cindy's box*, I thought. "I'm an *Examiner* man myself. So what?" I said.

"I think you know I'm a little sensitive as to who might be involved in this operation."

I did know. Bill Wethersby, in addition to being Hammersmith's antagonist, was also the city's most politically plugged-in defense attorney. He'd made his name by negotiating the freedom of eight hostages from a dinner party at the house of billionaire Karl Jentry. Last year, I'd stumbled into the fact that Wethersby had paid off the perpetrators, the New World Liberation Front, as part of those negotiations. Being the most celebrated and respected criminal attorney in town, he hadn't wanted his payoff to the NWLF to become public, so he did me a favor to bury the information. His presence now, outside my dilapidated apartment building, indicated that he wanted this information to remain buried.

"You aren't involved in this, are you?" I asked.

"Of course not. But I don't know who is, and I'd rather not read in the papers that it's somebody who could compromise me."

"I gave you all the incriminating evidence last year. Nobody can connect the dots without that," I said.

"Maybe."

"So what do you want from me?"

"Information. That's all. You mentioned last year that you found out about me from someone who dealt with the NWLF. I'd like to know if the NWLF is involved. If so, I'd need to start making preparations."

"You are one paranoid mother," I said.

"Thank you," he replied. "What do you think, can you help?"

45

"Out of the goodness of my heart?"

"I'd never have gotten anywhere relying on that from anyone. How about this?" He handed me an envelope with $200 in it. More money. More trouble.

"Just information?" I asked.

"All I want to know is if the people who are running the guns for Jim Jones can be linked back to me in any way. If they can't, then I'd prefer not to know anything about the matter at all."

I thought about Nelson's record collection sitting at the Record Exchange. "Deal." I shook his hand and grabbed the door handle. "Oh, I almost forgot. How's Miriam?"

Miriam was Wethersby's junkie daughter, who had become his life's cause. He'd become an expert on drug addiction in the process, raising millions for treatment, even opening a rehab clinic in Sonoma.

"Miriam is...okay. Thanks for asking." He looked at me with a mixture of deep sorrow and regret.

Never mind that he was one of the most prominent, unscrupulous political players in the city and that I couldn't even raise two nickels for my crippled best friend, I felt sorry for him. I hated myself for it, but goddamnit, I did.

11

Monday, August 28th, 7 p.m.

I exited Wethersby's car and returned to Cindy's place to collect the Jim Jones box I'd dismissed earlier in the day. As I approached Cindy's room for the second time that day, I saw a faint glow from underneath her apartment door. I scolded myself for leaving the light on, a cardinal sin for an apartment manager. I grabbed the door handle to insert the key and the room went dark. I hadn't forgotten to flip the light off; someone had remembered to flip it on. I pushed open the unlocked door and a shadow zipped into the bedroom.

"Come out," I said. I heard scuffling noises from behind the bedroom door. Whoever was in there wasn't trying to be quiet. "I'm opening the door," I shouted.

The commotion continued. I nudged the door open and saw a skinny teenager in jeans, a blue sweatshirt, and a blue knit cap on the floor rifling through Cindy's box of files on Jonestown.

"Hey," I said. The teenager ignored me and continued opening each folder, scanning its contents, then tossing it aside.

I took another step toward him and he jumped to his feet, pulling a switchblade from his back pocket. We stared at one another from five feet apart. I became disoriented looking at him, until I realized the reason why.

I wasn't staring at a teenage boy at all. I was facing off with the strangest looking woman I'd ever set eyes on, before or since. Her long, narrow face was youthful, pre-pubescent even, making her closely cropped, prematurely gray hair all the more striking. Her eyes were light brown, with flecks of gold. These features combined to give her a lithe, lupine appearance.

"Stay back," she said.

I put my hands up in an attempt to calm the situation. "Whatever you say," I said. "I don't want any trouble. You can walk right out of here."

"I'm taking these files," she said.

"Then we have a problem. What do you want with a bunch of old newspaper clippings anyway?"

"How do you know what's in here?" she asked.

"I'm not the one breaking into an apartment. You don't get to ask the questions. Now if you want to leave without a fuss, go right ahead."

"Okay," she said, and moved her knife toward her back pocket. I noticed she hadn't retracted the blade.

She lunged and swung the knife at my stomach. I hopped backward, grabbed Cindy's copy of *I'm Okay, You're Okay* off the desk, and threw it at my peculiar looking attacker. As she ducked, I rushed her, grabbed the knife and twisted the blade out of her hand. She hit me in the face with her left. Hell if she didn't throw a crisp punch, too.

Lucky for me, I'm a believer in equal rights, including her equal right to be hit back. I threw her against the wall headfirst and she collapsed to the floor. I assumed that was the end of it, but she bounced right up and took another run at me. I spun her around and wrapped her in a bear hug. She responded with a bite to my forearm.

"You're leaving me no choice," I said. She lowered her head and chomped on my index finger until it made a crunching sound. I wrenched her jaw open and threw her against the wall again, this time without regret.

She crumpled to the floor, and I was certain this time that was the end of it. But like a damn cat, she sprung over Cindy's bed. By the time I negotiated the desk chair and reached the other side of the room, she'd jumped out of the second story window.

A bone-cracking snap accompanied her landing on the cement. She boosted herself up and hobbled west on Pine. I sprinted down the stairs and out the front door, but she was already gone. Even with her most likely broken leg, I knew there was no use scouring the neighborhood for her. She'd have disappeared into one of the Tenderloin's many dark alleys. I returned to Cindy's room and cleaned it for the second time that day.

I carried Cindy's box of red Jonestown files back to the Crescent, and threw it into my room on the way upstairs to visit Nelson. He sat on his couch, staring vacantly at *The Gong Show*. I'd known Nelson now for over ten years and I'd never seen him depressed like this. Not by his crushed feet, not by a woman, not by poverty, not by anything.

I wrapped some ice in a paper towel and held it against my purple, crooked finger. I contemplated getting a rabies shot. I settled on a shot of Johnnie instead.

"What happened to you?" Nelson asked.

"Slammed a door on it," I replied, not wanting to bring Nelson's mood down anymore than it already was. "I got some good news and bad news for you, buddy."

"Yeah?" he said.

"Good news is I found your record collection."

He eyed me, bewildered. "Where is it?"

"The Record Exchange. Bill bought it this morning from some girl. He's holding it for you."

Nelson stood up to leave.

"You haven't heard the bad news," I said. "It's gonna cost two grand to get it back."

He sat back down. "Well, he might as well start selling it now. I got thirteen dollars to my name. It would take me ten years to raise that kind of extra cash."

"What if you started selling more weed?" I asked.

"What, stand out on the corner and sell dime bags? Shit, Sleeper, my feet wouldn't let me even if I wanted to. I sell to friends to pay the rent and to buy music and food. I got no interest in going to jail."

"Then we'll have to find another way."

"We?" he asked.

"Yeah, we. Believe it or not, two guys have given me a total of three hundred dollars."

"How we gonna turn three hundred into two thousand?"

"The old fashioned way," I said. "We'll gamble for it."

12

Tuesday, August 29ᵗʰ, 1 a.m.

Back in my room, I put on "Take me to the River" by the Talking Heads off their new album, *More Songs about Buildings and Food.*

I opened Cindy's box containing her Jim Jones files. They were organized in bright red file folders by year, starting in 1973 when she joined the Temple. There was lots of good press for Jones in the first few years. Jones protesting the tearing down of the International Hotel; Jones receiving the MLK Humanitarian award from Glide Memorial; Jones's appointment to the Housing Commission by Mayor Moscone; Temple services attended by every significant politician in town, all of whom elbowed one another out of the way in an attempt to be Jones's loudest cheerleader. Even First Lady Rosalynn Carter had held a private meeting with Jones during the presidential campaign.

Then, after an article in Rupert Murdoch's *New West* magazine appeared in '77, the dam surrounding Jones's lunacy began to crack. The *New West* article resounded throughout the city more than a similar one written by Les

Kingsolving for *The Examiner* a few years earlier, mainly because of its on-the-record details provided by ex-members like Cindy. There were reports of beatings, confiscation of member's assets, and sexual humiliation and perversity.

This exposé wasn't enough to rattle the politicians. After the article ran, Mayor Moscone released a statement saying he "will not conduct any investigation" because the article was "a series of allegations with absolutely no hard evidence that the Rev. Jones has violated any laws, either local, state or federal."

State Assemblyman Willie Brown one-upped Moscone in the ass-kissing department by describing Jones as "...a combination of Martin Luther King, Angela Davis, Albert Einstein, and Chairman Mao." Willie must not have seen Jim give him the middle finger behind his back one Sunday while Willie addressed the congregation.

Supervisor Harvey Milk wrote to President Carter in March of this year defending Jones and pleading to halt any investigation of the Temple. Milk specifically weighed in on a custody case involving one of the Temple's most public critics, ex-member Grace Stoen. Grace's son John remained in Guyana after Jones claimed paternity, a charge Grace vehemently denied. In his letter to Carter, Milk dismissed Grace as a blackmailer while calling Jones "...a man of the highest character" and a "...loving protective parent..." of John.

I know why the *New West* article didn't wake up the politicians; they would never alienate an active political constituency over one magazine article, no matter how bizarre or insidious that constituency was. But what about the rest of the city? Why hadn't this article pushed the rest of us to turn our backs on Jones?

The simple answer is that we didn't want to. The Peoples Temple was on the side of the poor, the disenfranchised, and the minority—all minorities. These were the people for whom the counter-cultural movement had fought. To turn their back on Jim Jones was to turn their back on themselves.

So what was my excuse? I'd dropped out of the hippie scene in '72, well before Jones came on the scene. I was proud of what we'd accomplished in the sixties, but I no longer held any illusions about our shortcomings, either.

What made my ambivalence toward Jones even worse was that I believed Cindy. Maybe not at first, but as soon as Jones and his followers hightailed it to Guyana, I knew Cindy was telling the truth. Prior to that move, I didn't have a strong opinion either way about Jones. Whatever floats your boat has always been my refrain. But moving your church halfway across the world because of one article in a small rag didn't seem like the actions of an innocent man to me.

And now, flipping through the articles in Cindy's box, Jones's madness was even more obvious. It's easy to gloss over this fact when you read one or two articles, sprinkled over months and years. But when they are all compiled in one place, it's harrowingly clear how insane he is.

My throat constricted when I read an article about how the Temple enforced secrecy among its members. I reread the offending sentence, shaken.

Hammersmith owed me more than one drink for the lie he'd told me at Donny's about the gold angel found on Cindy not meaning anything. For a deceit that big, he owed me at least a bottle.

13

The Golden Dragon Massacre trial was winding down at the Hall of Justice on Bryant Street. Hammersmith was assisting A.D.A. Levine in prosecuting four members of the Joe Boys gang who'd killed five innocent bystanders in a botched assassination attempt of rival gang leader, Michael "Hot Dog" Louie, at the Golden Dragon restaurant in Chinatown. Louie's nickname was so preposterous that it would have made me laugh if not for the five people who'd died in his wake.

I crammed into the last row of the courtroom and watched the proceedings. The defendant, Curtis Tam, was being questioned through an interpreter about his role in the massacre. From what I could decipher, he was claiming that the other shooters had threatened to kill him if he didn't participate. Apparently, the term "honor among thieves" didn't translate into Cantonese.

Hammersmith's bowtie and booming voice were perfect for the courtroom setting. I'd have been his pal no matter what, but it was still gratifying to see a friend excelling in his element.

"I didn't want to shoot nobody," Curtis Tam concluded his statement. His denial would have been more convincing to me if he hadn't unwittingly confessed his crime to an undercover Chinese cop in a Chinatown bar earlier in the year.

The judge called it a day and a bailiff escorted Tam back to jail. By the time the gallery poured out and Hammersmith had huddled in hushed tones with his colleagues, I was one of the few remaining people in the courtroom.

Hammersmith said goodbye to his co-workers and approached me in the last row.

"What's going on?"

"How could you not tell me the significance of the gold angel?" I asked.

He looked around at the nearly empty room. "Not the time or place, buddy."

"Come off it. Why didn't you tell me about the gold angel?"

"Jesus," he said, motioning me to the corner. "I guess this is going to be the time and place."

We sat down near the wall, each of us relaxing a touch.

"I bought you a drink, didn't I?" Hammersmith said.

"This is a rare case where that's not good enough," I said.

"So I'm clear, what exactly are you talking about?"

"I'm doing some research on the Temple and a *Chronicle* article reported that ex-members are concerned about retaliation from the Temple's security arm. Concerned, as in, concerned for their lives."

"Could be paranoia."

"Don't bullshit me. You know it's not. The article also reports that the security arm of the Temple is called The

Angels. Why didn't you tell me?"

"I didn't want to scare you. It *could* be a coincidence," he said.

"Has anyone else been killed?"

"What?"

"Has anyone else been killed?" I repeated.

"Not lately."

"Not *lately*? What the hell does that mean?" I asked.

"Does the name Bob Houston ring a bell?" he whispered.

"No. Why should it?"

"He was a Temple member who tried to leave in nineteen seventy-six. Bob was supposed to meet his ex-wife Joyce, who'd left the Temple a few years before, in Ohio. He never made it there."

"What happened?" I asked.

"The day he defected he was found dead on the Southern Pacific railroad in Portrero Hill."

"And his killers?" I asked.

"Never found."

"Why'd they let his wife go and not him?"

"Joyce split a few years back, before the craziness kicked into full gear," Hammersmith replied. "Also, could be because Bob was a Temple officer who knew things that a run-of-the-mill member wouldn't."

"Why wasn't anyone arrested?"

"We tried. It's not easy to penetrate a cult."

"You still don't think they could have killed Cindy?" I asked.

"My money's on George."

"Not mine."

"Then spend your time exonerating George. But don't

go screwing with the Temple. Its reach is longer than you think."

"They're in Guyana for fuck's sake," I said.

"Like I said, it's longer than you think."

14

Wednesday, September 6th, 4 p.m.

Hammersmith, of all people, should have known the quickest way to get me to do something was to tell me not to do it. So he thought George killed Cindy. The police thought so, too. As did Simon. So why didn't I? Because I agreed with Desma, that Cindy and George loved one another, as Willie Nelson would say, "in their own peculiar way."

I took BART over to Berkeley to find some answers about the Temple at the Human Freedom Center. The Center was a run-down, former nursing home founded by Jeannie and Al Mills, Temple defectors who had changed their names from Deanna and Elmer Mertle. The center was a meeting place for the Concerned Relatives, former Temple members who, in addition to supporting one another, worked to free their friends and family who wanted out of Guyana.

I zigzagged up its front ramp and rang the doorbell. The handle jiggled from the inside and the door cracked open. A small, anxious, librarian of a woman peeked her head out. "May I help you?" she asked.

"Hi." I didn't know what to say. "I was a friend of Cindy

Teague."

"Oh, dear. Please come in," the librarian said. "I'll go get Jeannie."

The entry room was filled with furniture that looked like what you would think leftovers from a nursing home would: old and cranky. The off-white walls were bare and scuffed, the light brown carpet worn thin.

A man and woman emerged from the back offices, and to my surprise, my focus was drawn to the man. In my defense, it's not every day you see someone wearing an eye patch and a pinstripe suit. Whispering, the two shook hands goodbye, and Sir Cyclops departed.

After the front door closed behind him, the woman turned to me. "Hi, I'm Jeannie." Jeannie was a striking woman with dark feathered hair, prominent eyebrows, and deep brown, alert eyes. She smiled and her deep dimples gave her an impish, chipmunk quality. "What can I do for you?" she asked.

"I was a friend of Cindy Teague," I repeated.

"Such a tragedy." She grabbed both my hands and fixed her eyes on mine. "How can we help you?"

"I don't know. I'm feeling a little lost after her death. I know she spent a lot of time over here and I wanted to learn more about this part of her life."

"About what part of her life?" she asked.

"The Temple. Her sister."

"I see. Why don't you come back to my office, Mister..."

"Hayes. But nobody calls me that. Call me Sleeper."

"Okay, Sleeper."

I followed her through a series of narrow, ramshackle rooms containing equally shabby furnishings. Jeannie's office was no exception, holding a serviceable desk and a couple of creaky chairs.

"So tell me what you really want, Sleeper," she said.

"What do you mean?"

"I spent six years with Jim Jones, the biggest liar on the planet. I've become something of an expert."

"I'm not lying. I was a friend of Cindy's. I want to know about the Temple," I said.

"And what else?" she asked.

I saw no point in holding back. "I want to know if they were involved in her death."

She stood up and closed the door. "Involved how?" she asked.

"Involved, as in killed her."

"Why would you think that?"

"Because I don't know who else it could have been," I said.

"Again with the half-truths?" she asked.

"Fine. I know a few things about the circumstances of her death that the public doesn't know. It's a wild theory, but I want to know if murder is something within the Temple's capabilities."

"Why don't you tell me the circumstances and I'll tell you what they are capable of," she said.

"The police found a gold angel on her body."

"A gold angel?" she asked.

"Yes."

"Oh. That is troubling," she said.

"You think it could be the work of their security arm?"

"The Angels were all of our first thought when we heard about her murder," she replied.

"*Our?*"

"All of us who left the Temple. The Concerned Relatives."

"You're going to have to explain what went on at the Temple to me. Why do all of you need a support group? Why can't people leave if they want to? This is all very confusing to a card-carrying atheist."

She closed her eyes and cringed. When she opened them again, I saw her full, undiluted pain. "Do you want to know why Al and I decided to leave the Temple?" she asked.

"If you want to tell me."

"Because Jim Jones decided that my nine-year-old daughter needed to be beaten seventy times with a paddle in front of the Temple congregation for talking with another girl that Jim disapproved of. A supposed lesbian, he claimed."

"That's horrible. He's a freak. I get it. I still don't understand why members just don't leave if it's so bad, or why the Temple would want to kill anyone who does manage to escape."

"Are you doing anything the rest of the night?"

"Nothing that can't wait," I said.

"Then I'd like you to stay for our weekly meeting of Concerned Relatives. I think you'll get a much better understanding of what we're dealing with after that."

"Sure," I said. "Can I ask you something else?"

"Please."

"Who was Rooster Cogburn?"

Not a John Wayne fan, she stared at me, perplexed.

"The guy with the eye-patch?" I clarified.

"Oh. That was Joe Mazor. He's a P.I. who represents us in our negotiations with the Temple."

I remembered his name from Cindy's newspaper clippings. "What are you negotiating?" I asked.

"The release of our loved ones."

"But—"

"It will all be a lot clearer to you after the meeting."

After I killed a few hours on Telegraph Avenue, Jeannie began the Concerned Relatives meeting at 7 p.m. sharp, introducing me as "a friend of Cindy's," a simple description the group accepted without reservation. Al, Jeannie's amiable husband and former Temple photographer, shook my hand with an exuberant, bone-crushing grip, exacerbating the pain of my recently gnawed finger.

I met Wanda, whose 12-year-old boy was in Jonestown. She told me that she, like many other members, had been forced to sign false documents stating that Jones was the child's father, making the legal recourse to bring her son home next to impossible.

I met Grace Stoen, the woman Supervisor Harvey Milk had defamed in his letter to President Carter. I would've liked to have met Grace, with her sultry Mediterranean features, under better circumstances. As it was, the setting couldn't have been worse. She described to me how she had signed a blank piece of paper that became another statement of Jones's paternity. As a result, her son was also stranded in Guyana without either of his genetic parents.

I met Neva, whose husband was part of Jones's personal security detail. She told me about the Temples' plots to either kidnap the children of politicians who were disloyal to the Temple, or if that wasn't plausible, to kill them.

One thing they all agreed on was their fear of Temple retribution. The Temple subjected all of its members to physical harm for the slightest transgression. For a major offense, such as defection, the penalty was rumored to be death.

"So is there such thing as the Angels?" I asked.

"Most definitely," Grace said. "It's headed by this masochist woman. Nobody knows her name."

The lights flickered on and off. Not uncommon for old buildings in the Bay Area during a rainstorm.

"She's a fanatic," Jeannie said. "Crazy looking. One hundred and twenty pounds of skin and bone."

"She sleeps in a damn closet," Wanda said.

"Gray hair, light brown, almost yellow eyes?" I asked.

"Yeah. How did you know?" Grace replied.

"I caught her breaking into Cindy's apartment. We had a lively discussion," I said, holding up my still-mangled index finger. "How did all of you get involved with the Temple in the first place? You all seem so normal. More normal than me, at least," I said.

"When you join it's very idealistic. Our causes were racial and economic equality. You feel like you're fighting the good fight," Grace said. "Then the beatings start, and the humiliation, and the paranoia. It doesn't happen all at once. It's baby steps, until you're so far in the woods you can't make sense of anything."

The room fell quiet. Nobody looked at one another. I'd never seen a more scared, wounded bunch of people in my life. I went there wondering if Jones was capable of killing Cindy. Now I was certain he was capable of much worse.

"Can I ask you a question?" Wanda asked me.

"Sure," I said. After they opened themselves up to me, I was in no position to deny them anything, though I had become distracted by an unpleasant odor in the room.

"Why are you here? Is there something you know about Cindy's death?"

I knew I had to tell them about the gold angel, even if it magnified their already palpable fear. "When the police found Cindy," I started, "there was a gold angel on top her body." Their faces dropped. "It could mean nothing. The police have other suspects."

"But you don't believe those other suspects are guilty?" Wanda asked.

"No. But that doesn't matter much. I'm wrong about most things," I said, trying to downplay what I'd told them. A couple of them managed a polite smile. "If you all think The Angels are trying to kill you, then why are you risking your lives?"

"Same reason as Cindy," Wanda said. "We want our loved ones back from Guyana."

"We're close to getting Congressman Ryan to schedule a visit," Grace added. "I plan on going with him and bringing back as many as I can. The better question is, why are *you* risking *your* life?"

Until that moment, I hadn't realized I was.

I breathed in, digesting this alarming fact, when my apartment manager instincts kicked in. I connected the lights flickering—there wasn't any rainstorm—with the odd smell of plastic burning.

"Everyone get out," I exclaimed. They stared at me, confused. "There's an electrical fire somewhere in the house. Where's your fuse box?" I asked Jeannie.

"Around back."

"Out the front. Now."

One good thing about cult members, they do what they're told. When we reached the front door, we found it blocked from the outside with something. I rushed to open a window, but was unsurprised to find it painted shut.

"Al, throw a chair through the window and help everyone out. Then find a phone and call the fire department. Jeannie, show me where the electrical box is," I ordered.

Jeannie and I ran to the back where I also used a chair to knock out a window. I slid out first, slashing my back in the process. Jeannie, being much smaller, jumped out unscathed.

The electrical box was sparking, as was an outdoor light connected to the house. I did the math and it equaled two pennies. Somebody had jammed one penny behind the light itself and another behind its corresponding fuse.

"Do you have a shovel?" I asked.

"In the garage."

"Go get it."

She returned and I scooped a shovelful of dirt on the electrical box. I did it again, and again, until there were no visible sparks. I shut off the main circuit breaker by throwing a large rock on it, then smashed the light fixture on the side of the house with the same rock.

The source of the fire was now cut off. The remaining question was how far the fire was spreading between the walls and whether or not the fire department could contain it.

We waited out front most of the night for the firemen to do their job. Jeannie was lucky. The fire had reached no further than the back room where the wiring to the outdoor light was located. The place would smell terrible for a while, and the back walls would need replacing. But other than that, the house would be livable.

65

"Sleeper," Jeannie hugged me, "thank you for saving us."
"Before I came here I thought you were all being paranoid."
"And now?"
"All too sane."

15

Thursday, September 7th, 6 p.m.

I was more convinced than ever that Cindy's death was related to the Temple somehow. That wouldn't stop Simon, however, from administering his own brand of justice on George if I couldn't find any evidence exonerating him. Talking with George about Cindy wouldn't be easy, but if it meant saving him from Simon's vengeance, then George and I were both going to have to endure one hell of an uncomfortable conversation.

I rode the 47 Van Ness bus across town to Local 261's offices at 18th and Shotwell. A handful of black workers were setting up folding chairs in the main hall in preparation for a union meeting. Their race was notable because of 261's recent history of intra-union feuding between its black and Chicano membership. George had won his election by cobbling a coalition between the white and black factions, which was how, prior to his arrest, Buster Lemmer had become second in command.

"George around?" I asked one of the workers.

"He's at dinner. Be back in a little bit."

"What time is the meeting?"

"Eight o'clock."

I looked at the clock on the wall. It was almost six. "Can you tell him Sleeper Hayes is waiting for him at Cribbins?"

"You got it," he answered.

An hour later, George sat down next to me and ordered a club soda from Old Man Cribbins, who'd operated the bar, while living in the upstairs apartment, since 1909. I took note of George's drink, not his usual Stoli on the rocks with a twist.

He noticed my look of surprise at his drink order. "Got a union meeting in a little bit. Can't show up with liquor on my breath. Especially not now." He swished the ice around in his drink. Despite his troubles, he still dressed like he was performing *Guys and Dolls* on Broadway. His light blue silk suit with quarter-inch stripes matched his black bowler hat and tie. He was one of the last men left in America who wore a pocket watch without irony. "Plus, I've backed off the hooch since Cindy was killed. I assume that's why you're here, about Cindy?"

"To Cindy," I said, raising my glass.

"'There is special providence in the fall of a sparrow,'" he added.

Goddamned Shakespeare, always stealing everyone else's thunder.

"So whatsup, Sleeper? I have to get back for the meeting."

Better to rip the Band-Aid off right away than drag this out. "We go back a little ways, right?" I asked. "I mean we're not best friends, but you've always shot straight with me."

"And you with me, Sleeper. What's going on?"

"I got a friend in the D.A.'s office. He says they're looking

68

at you for Cindy's murder," I said.

"That's no secret. It's been in all the papers. The police questioned me already. What's your point?"

I hated myself for what I was about to do, the worst thing you can do to other human beings: manipulate them.

"I know something that's not in the papers," I said.

"What's that?"

"They found blood at the scene that wasn't hers," I lied.

"So what?"

"So, when they find out what type, they might be knocking on your door."

"The D.A. is saying it's my type?"

"In so many words." I watched his reaction, looking for a tell that never came.

"'Done to death by slanderous tongue.'" George swallowed the rest of his club soda. "First of all, it's not my blood. I'll give you a pint right now if you don't believe me. Second, even if they told you that, it's a set-up. The D.A.'s office is cooperating with Justice on their investigation of me. And third, what the fuck business is it of yours?"

Screw me. So he didn't know.

"I'm sorry, George. I had to make sure you didn't kill her. Some people at the Triangle were starting to believe the worst of you. Believe it or not, I was the one on your side."

"So there was no blood?"

"Not that I know of."

"Fuck you, Sleeper." He stood up to leave.

"George, don't be pissed. You *were* the last one to see her alive."

"No, I wasn't. She was going to meet some reporter after our date. But then again, I told the police that already."

"What was she talking to a reporter about?"

"What do you think? That deviant Jim Jones. Goodbye, Sleeper. I have work to do. Don't bother me with your bullshit again."

Christ. I had to do it to be sure, for George's sake. Just like I had to keep drinking, for my own sake, to forget I'd done it.

16

Friday, September 8th, 2 a.m.

I stumbled out of Cribbins at closing, my brain too scrambled to figure out the best Muni route back home. A brown Pinto pulled onto the sidewalk in front of me, rescuing me from my confusion. Two behemoths who looked a little like construction workers and a lot like The Village People got out and blocked my path. Both of them were taller than my 6'2" frame and twice as wide.

"Get in the car," the shorter of the two giants said.

"No thanks, Macho Man," I replied.

"We're not asking, Hayes. Get in."

They shoved me into the backseat of the car, peeled down Mission, hung a left on South Van Ness, across Market Street, and stopped right in front of the Federal Building. The alcohol was wreaking havoc with my sense of déjà vu. They yanked me out of the car and into the elevator.

"I already talked to your boss last week," I blathered, before noting that the elevator hadn't stopped on the 12th floor like it had last time.

"Let's go," the little giant said.

I wasn't escorted to a cozy conference room this time, either. I was placed, instead, in a small, gloomy interrogation room. The floors were concrete and the windows, despite our elevation, were adorned with iron bars. The big giant pulled a pair of real handcuffs from his fake construction belt and cuffed me to a tiny table affixed to the floor.

"Wait here," Little Giant ordered, before leaving the room with his band mate.

"Good idea," I responded to nobody in particular. I had to piss in the way that only drinking two gallons of Budweiser can make you feel, making the ten-minute wait seem like an hour. At last, a normal-sized human in a suit walked in flanked by his henchman, looking like the worst cover band of all time.

"I'm Investigator Hackett with the Justice Department. You've already met my colleagues," he began.

"Can't miss those two," I said.

"Actually, you did. They're part of the undercover team monitoring George Urbancyck. They're dressed this way to blend in at George's hangouts."

"Where's George hanging out, Moby Dicks?" I said, referencing a popular gay bar in the Castro. But he was right. I hadn't noticed them at Cribbins. "Speaking of dicks, I have to take a piss," I said.

"In time. We brought you in here because we saw you meeting with Urbancyck tonight."

"I can't have a drink with a friend without being arrested?" I asked.

"You're not arrested, Mr. Hayes."

"Could have fooled me," I said, yanking on my handcuffs.

"You usually drink with George at the Triangle," he said,

ignoring my rattling. "Why the change of venue? And why did you go to the union offices first?"

Was the entire city crawling with Feds investigating something or other?

"Screw off," I said. "I'm no snitch."

"What would you be snitching about? Cindy Teague's murder?"

"I thought you were investigating George for the union's finances. Isn't murder the police's beat?"

"When one of our informants is strangled, we take a particular interest in the investigation," he replied.

"Informant? Who?"

"Cindy Teague."

"Bullshit. Why would she do that?" I asked, trying to cover my genuine surprise.

"Because she wanted our help getting her sister out of Guyana. She was a little obsessed with that, as I'm sure you know."

"And you guys couldn't help her out unless she gave you something on George in return?"

"Why don't you tell us why you were meeting with Urbancyck tonight."

"George didn't kill anyone. You're wasting your time. Now can I piss or not?"

"We don't think George killed Cindy. We're thinking someone might have done it for him."

"Like who?" I slurred, then spat what little bit of sticky saliva I could gather in my mouth.

"I don't know, you, perhaps," he answered.

"You're insane," I said.

"Really?"

"Really. I have an alibi for that night," I said.

"How convenient."

"Yeah, I was right in this building down a few floors with your colleagues from the FBI. You guys should talk in the elevator once in a while."

Hackett unsuccessfully tried to hide his embarrassment for not knowing this crucial little detail about my whereabouts the night of the murder.

"So," I continued, seizing the upper hand, "George and me are all in it together somehow? That's your theory? And you wonder why nobody believes the Warren Commission."

"It would be much better for you if you come clean now, than to make us go through all the paces, only to snatch you up later."

"I don't believe any of this," I said. "George is a stand-up guy." Though I had to admit that if what Hackett was saying about Cindy cooperating was true, and if George had found out, it did change the math more than a little bit.

"Urbancyck may or may not have had that girl killed, but I can assure you of one thing, he is not a stand-up guy. He's as crooked as Lombard Street," he said.

"Well, I didn't kill anyone. Now, I'm about to piss all over this floor. Unless you or The Village People are hell bent on mopping up urine, I'd uncuff me."

Hackett let out the exasperated exhale I'd perfected in eliciting from people. "Take 'em off," he said to the giants. "And let him stumble home."

17

Friday, September 8th, 10 a.m.

I awoke the next day with the acrid tang of hangover in my mouth. I swallowed hard, my stomach begrudgingly accepting the viscous saliva. This was not going to be a routine hangover cured by a shower and a mug of coffee. This one was going to be a daylong battle.

Luckily, I don't mind devastating hangovers as much as most people. Severe hangovers give me a singular purpose otherwise lacking in my life: make it through the day. If I can accomplish even the most mundane tasks, then I am a wild success. Some might say heroic. Much to my consternation, my ex-wife never saw it that way. Of course, that was because I never revealed the true extent of my pain. Had she known my condition, perhaps she'd have been much more impressed by me taking out the garbage or washing the dishes. Living by the warrior's code of silence, though, I never received my proper recognition.

After a couple of dry heaves, I staggered down to the basement to empty the garbage chutes. Over the past few years, Jake, the owner, and I had upgraded the Crescent from war-torn to merely earthquake-ravaged. We traded a couple of hookers, a skinhead speed freak, and a violent, unstable married couple for Nelson and the Phams, a family of Vietnamese immigrants. We rented out another apartment to a revolving door of Merchant Marines who used it when they were on leave. Ernie Mack in 3C was a holdover who kept to himself and always paid his rent on time. I suspected he kept a low profile because he was involved in something illicit and didn't want to attract attention to himself.

Another holdover was Lady Ellinger. Despite her nickname, Lady was not the prim and proper type. She yelled and cussed like a sailor, most of the time directing her profanity at me. She'd earned her regal title instead for her prolonged tenure in the Crescent, dating back to the late fifties. Though she was hard on me, having Lady in the building had its benefits. She observed the daily comings and goings on Hyde Street from her second floor window, reporting on any suspicious characters or activity. In the T.L. that made for a full-time job.

After collecting the garbage, I battled my way to Newman's. Billy was taking his customary nap on the bleachers, the racing form a thin blanket. My heavy footsteps bounced him awake.

"I got us a bet," he said, opening one eye.

"Sweet music. Let's hear it." Nelson's records were collecting dust at the Record Exchange.

"The Bay Meadows Futurity runs today. You look horrible, by the way, Sleeper."

"Long night."

"What's new?" he asked.

"Fine, longer night. Since when did you start playing

76

quarter horses?" I asked.

"Since Lukas decided to stop," Billy said.

"I'm not following you."

D. Wayne Lukas was a trainer who had dominated quarter horse racing the last few years in Northern California. He'd recently announced his intention to drop quarter horses and exclusively train the more lucrative thoroughbreds by the end of '78.

"D. Wayne has already sold off most of his quarter horses, right?" Billy asked

"If you say so."

"I say so. All he has left is his first team. Except for this one here. Look." He pointed to the form. "There is no reason this nag should still be in his barn, much less entered in the Futurity."

"Let me see." I snatched the form from him. Sure enough, *Some Romance* looked to be the slowest horse entered, by a lot. For gamblers, this scenario is known as the logic of illogic. D. Wayne must have been holding on to this plodder for a reason, even if that reason wasn't apparent anywhere in the racing form.

"You have my attention. You got a morning line?" I asked.

"Twenty to one."

"Let's do it," I said.

Billy handed me a twenty. "All to win," he said.

"You sure you don't want to go across the board?" I nudged him.

"Don't start with me, Sleeper. You know my rules."

"I'll walk it down to Dmitri later," I said.

I turned my focus to the boxing ring, where Ricky was holding the mitts for Alfredo and cussing up a storm. I hadn't heard Ricky get on Alfredo like that since Alfredo was an amateur.

"You're sloppy, Fredo. You're sloppy," he yelled. "Stay down on your turn. You stand up every time. Get the weight on the back foot, then punch. Don't cock it back. Don't fucking cock it back! Just let it out. Stop, stop, stop! What is wrong with you? The fight's in a week and you're getting lazy. What the hell's going on?"

"Nothing, man. I'm tired. Let me rest for five minutes and we'll pick it back up," Alfredo said.

"Rest? You think you can rest once the bell rings? That's not how it works, Alfredo. Let's go. Now. Come on. And don't stand up! Snap it. Snap it!"

"What's going on over there?" I asked Billy. "Alfredo doesn't look *that* off."

Billy shrugged his shoulders. "Been this way for a couple of days. Alfredo's been a little slow and Ricky's been relentless with him."

"That's not like Alfredo. The guy loves to train," I said.

"I'll try and talk to him without Ricky around. See if he'll open up to me."

"Alright. I'm off to Dmitri's to get us down on this race."

"Tell Dmitri to kiss my Irish ass," Billy said.

"It almost goes without saying."

"Almost," Billy laughed.

I shuffled down Eddy Street and found Dmitri sitting in his back booth at the Acropolis Café reading, like always, a book on American history. This one was about Dwight Eisenhower.

"Did you know Eisenhower smoked four packs of cigarettes a day?" Dmitri asked.

"Better than eating that crap," I replied, nodding at his plate of tabouleh. "How can you stand it? Stuff tastes like dirt mixed with dirt."

"The wife says it's good for the digestive system." He wiped his mouth with a napkin. "What do you want?"

"I want forty to win and twenty to place and show on *Some Romance* in the Bay Meadows Futurity."

"Quarter horses? Not my thing," Dmitri responded.

"You're a bookie, remember. That's your job. To book bets."

"What's the morning line?" he asked.

"Twenty to one."

"Fine. It's booked," he said.

"You might want to lay a little of this off. I think he's got a real shot," I said.

"Okay. Thanks for the heads-up. Anything else?"

"Yeah, you can give my seat up for tonight's card game." I waited for Dmitri's standard joke.

"Hot date?"

And there it was, right on cue.

"Nah. I gotta check in on someone."

"Okay, see you soon."

"See you tomorrow, you mean," I replied. Dmitri looked befuddled. "I'll be back to pick up my winnings on *Some Romance*."

18

Friday, September 8th, 1 p.m.

I actually had to check in on two people. The first visit was a personal one that was starting to feel a little like business; the second was business that, with a little luck, would turn out personal.

Lori opened the door on my first knock this time, wearing a yellow and white-striped sweater with bell-bottom jeans. She looked better, sober.

"How you doing?" I asked.

"I'm good. Thanks for taking care of me yesterday. I'm feeling better. A *lot* better," she replied.

"Yeah?" I said.

"Seriously. I'm gonna go to a meeting tonight before work and everything. What are you up to?"

"I have to take BART over to Oakland to see someone but I wanted to ask you a question first," I said. "What do you know about Cindy's sister?"

"Janice? In Guyana?"

"I was thinking about digging around, trying to get her out."

"That's sweet of you. What do you want to know?"

"Let's start with whether she even wants out," I said.

"All I know is what Cindy told me, which was that she did. But that stays between us."

"What do you mean?" I asked.

"Maybe I'm being paranoid, but I'd rather not be on the Temple's radar, at all. Cindy said they didn't tolerate criticism from defectors."

"Defectors? What is this, the Soviet Union?" I asked. "Of course I won't tell anyone. Do you remember anything else Cindy said about Janice?"

"Not that I can remember," she said.

"Okay. I should be home by nine o'clock or so. Stop by after work?"

"You gonna remember me this time?"

"How could I forget?"

"I don't know, but somehow you find a way," she said.

"Not tonight. I've got some tricks I've been holding back for a special occasion."

"Ooh, sounds fun. But do me one favor, Mr. Magician."

"What's that?" I asked.

"No hats, no rabbits, no assistants."

"I promise," I said, "absolutely nothing."

I hadn't done any digging for Wethersby yet on the Temple's gun running operation and I knew he'd be getting impatient. I hoped my second appointment could shed some light on the matter. I called Tenora Percy from a payphone at Hyde and Grove, before descending into the Civic Center BART station. Her mother assured me she'd be back in an hour.

I hopped off at Fruitvale in Oakland, doubled back to

19th street, crossed East 14th Street, and stopped in front of a small white house with green trim. There was a short, decorative three-foot fence in front that would neither prevent an intruder from breaking in, nor keep a child from breaking out.

Tenora's four-year-old son, Jamal, answered the door. He was a foot taller since the last time I saw him over a year ago. I thought there was a glint of recognition in his eyes until he yelled out, "Hey Mama, some white man's at the door."

"Jamal!" Tenora snapped, shooing him away. "I'm sorry, Sleeper. He knows better than that."

"No need to apologize. His description was right on the nose."

"A little too on the nose. Remember, his father is some white man, too," she said, referring to our mutual friend and hippie royalty, Diamond Dan Watson. "Come on in," she continued. "Can I get you something to drink? There's a couple of Millers in the fridge."

"You having one?"

"No, I've got to study," she replied.

"Great. I'll take them both." I smiled to let her in on the joke. "One will do fine."

"Okay. Let's go out back," she said.

We walked through the front hallway and cramped kitchen in about six steps, exiting into a back area that I couldn't call a yard, given its lack of grass. The space was barely large enough to fit a metal table and chairs, a grill, and little Jamal's Big Wheel. Jamal picked up a whiffle ball and threw it against the wood fence, imitating Vida Blue's high leg kick.

I think I could call Tenora a friend by this time. It hadn't always been that way. In the sixties, we had spent most of our time together at each other's throats. Me, about her hardline radical beliefs, and she, about my "unseriousness" to "the cause." Her militant attitude and my apathy eventually caused a sizable fissure in our relationship.

Then last year, we were thrown together under the same roof. By then, she had become disillusioned with the black radical movement and took up with Diamond Dan. During our time together, we had a flirtation, a falling out, and a reconciliation. Soon after, realizing that she was even less suited for the hippie scene than she was for the militant one, she enrolled at Hastings Law School and moved back in with her mom.

From the looks of it, she was inching toward her real self. No more tight afros and military berets, no more Rasta dreads and tie-dyes. Her hair was a conservative, medium length. She wore a utilitarian sweater over a pair of tight designer jeans, a style that, much to my approval, was starting to infringe on the bell-bottom's decade-long dominance. She also looked like she had lost about ten pounds of her baby weight.

"How's the view, Sleeper?" she asked, interrupting my ogling.

"Good," I said. "You look good. Are you?"

"I don't have time to think like that. Between law school, work, and Jamal, all I think about is sleep." She yawned and rubbed her eyes, emphasizing the point. "How about you, you good?"

"Can't complain. Drawing more aces than deuces."

"You're still pretending you don't care about anything?"

Tenora, like most women I've met, had the faulty impression that there is more to me than drinking and gambling. Every now and then, especially if I'm trying to get them into bed, I'll let them think it awhile. Sooner or later, the truth dawns on all of them. All of them, I guess, except Tenora.

"Sports, politics, same thing," I replied.

"How's that?"

"Pick a team and root like hell."

"Funny," she said.

"I'm serious. The difference is I can make money off sports. The only people making money off politics are the politicians."

"Then why are you here? No money to be made at my house," she said.

"I was wondering if you could help me with some information. Have you read this stuff about the Peoples Temple smuggling guns into Guyana?" I asked.

"And you thought of me. How flattering."

"You did swim in those waters," I said.

"Previous life. How can I help?"

"I'm wondering if you know who might be helping them," I said.

"Anyone in particular?"

"Two. The NWLF and Janks."

Curtis Janko, or Janks, was a former hippie turned gun dealer whom Tenora and I both knew. He had the same connection that could lead back to Wethersby, namely he'd laundered money through the guy Wethersby used to pay off the NWLF.

Janks and I never got along, even back in the sixties. Another example of how in relationships, personality trumps ideology. Just because we vote the same way doesn't mean

I want to have a beer with you. And it definitely doesn't mean I will give you a pass if you're selling guns to the Peoples Temple.

"Hmm. This is no good," she replied.

"Why's that?"

"Before we talk about Curtis, let me say I'd rule out the NWLF. Neither they, nor Jim Jones, are what I'd call team players."

"But Janks?" I said.

"What makes you think he's involved, anyway?"

"I remember he was helping the Temple set up camp in Guyana last year."

"How is your memory so good with all the alcohol you drink?" she asked.

"I find that one tends to remember things when staring down the barrel of a gun."

"I could see how that could make an impression," she said.

"So, Janks, what do you know?"

She grabbed the beer out of my hand, took a sip, and handed it back. I followed her sip with one of my own. I smelled her lipstick on the bottle and, for a second, my mind wandered to a simpler place.

"He could be helping them, I guess," she said. "I heard he was asking around about buying some guns a while back. I didn't think much of it at the time. Why do you care, anyway?"

"You want to be in the position of knowing something about this?"

She looked at me, amused. Or bemused. I'm not sure. Definitely mused in some way. "No, I don't," she decided.

"I didn't think so. Is Janks still living with Diamond Dan?"

"No. He moved out about the time I did. He's crashing in the city at a warehouse South of Market. Seventh and Harrison, I think."

"Thanks, Tenora."

"I'll make a call on the NWLF, too."

"You got my number, right?"

"Yep, and I know where you live," she replied.

"You know, I'm still waiting for another at bat," I said.

"It's not my fault you struck out the first time. Anyway, I'm out of the game for now."

"They don't call me 'The Comeback Kid' for nothing," I said.

"Does anyone really call you that?"

"Absolutely."

"Seriously?"

"Maybe."

"Really?"

"Never."

19

Friday, September 8th, 4 p.m.

I BARTed back to San Francisco, content that at least one person I knew had their life on the right track.

Wethersby would be relieved that the NWLF wasn't involved in the Jim Jones gun running investigation. They were the one direct link to his past. Janks was a peripheral threat, at most. Someone would have to do extraordinary detective work and know precisely what to look for in order to find Wethersby's payoff from the NWLF through Janks.

Still, Wethersby was a thorough man and I knew he expected me to run down every loose ball. This was one grounder I didn't relish chasing. The main bone of contention between Janks and me during the sixties was that Janks was a complete and utter asshole. Confronting him about running guns was not how I'd envisioned spending my Friday night.

I exited the BART at the San Francisco Civic Center and headed south on 10th to Harrison. It took me half an hour to figure out which run-down, abandoned warehouse was Janks's.

I banged on its faded gray metal door. The rattle echoed down an alley lined with broken bottles and discarded syringes. I peeked through a dusty window. Apart from a mattress on the floor and a hot plate next to it, the warehouse was empty.

I kept pounding until I was satisfied nobody was there. I punched out a small, thin window on the side of the building, unlocked the latch, and slid the window up. Not quite Fort Knox in its security.

"Yo, Janks!" I called out. No answer.

There was a sheetless mattress on the floor surrounded by a handful of roaches in an ashtray, a *Guardian*, some revolutionary tripe by Chomsky, and a *Hustler*. Definitely Janks's pad.

The rest of the place was deserted. There wasn't even any detritus of day-to-day living. No dirty clothes, leftover food, or used toiletries. I didn't see a bathroom, either. It looked more like an emergency crash pad to me, not a regular place of residence.

I noticed a newly constructed ladder at the back of the warehouse ascending to a small loft. I climbed to the top, conceding with every step on its sturdy rungs that Janks's carpentry skills were first-rate. When I reached the top of the loft, I saw three wooden, six feet long crates pushed back against the wall. Even though I knew what I would find inside, I pried the top off of one to be certain. Sure enough, it contained four rifles, broken down into parts. It didn't take a gun enthusiast to know that these weren't hunting rifles, either. As far as I had strayed from the peace and love idealism of the sixties, Janks had strayed even further.

The lack of personal belongings in the warehouse made

more sense. Janks must have crashed here only when guns were onsite. Made me wonder why he wasn't here now. As soon as that thought flashed in my mind, the door clattered open.

I peeked over the front of the loft and saw Janks walk in holding a paper deli bag. He sat down on the mattress, unwrapped a sandwich, and took a ravenous bite.

My first instinct was to wait him out, but the more I thought about it, the more I decided against it. What if the gun deal was going down soon? What if he decided to check on the merchandise? Sometimes doing nothing is more risky than taking action. Or, in sports terminology, sometimes the best defense is a good offense.

Aware that every little noise would echo in the vast warehouse, I slid to the back of the loft, lifted myself onto my knees, still below Janks's sightline, and surveyed my options. There was an adjoining building ten feet below this one. Jumping onto it wasn't a possibility. If Janks didn't hear the window open, he'd hear me land on the metal roof.

There was another, larger window on the opposite wall. I slipped off my workboot and rose back to my knees. Holding my boot by the top like an ax, I threw it, end over end, at the window. I would have missed high if I hadn't misjudged the distance, a good fifteen feet farther than I had thought. The window, being old and brittle, didn't make the deafening sound I'd hoped. Janks, looking more annoyed than startled, continued chewing his sandwich. After finishing his bite, he reluctantly rose to investigate.

As soon as he opened the front door, I scurried across the loft, threw up the back window, and lowered myself down onto the adjoining roof. I ran across the hot metal, my shoeless left foot burning with every step, and jumped onto the fire escape. I made my way down the swaying ladder, then turned down the alley toward 8th Street.

"Missing something?" a familiar voice asked.

I turned around and there he was, holding up my boot. "You know, I've been wondering where that old thing was hiding. Thanks, Janks," I replied.

He wasn't amused, though to be fair, he rarely was. He looked about how he did the last time I saw him over a year ago, lean and muscular. His short-cropped hair had grown out to Beatles length, circa Abbey Road, and the crazy glint in his eye had grown larger, threatening to usurp the lucid portion entirely.

"What are you doing here, Sleeper? Why did you break into my place?"

"It was already well-broken," I said. "I just rearranged it a little."

"Stop the nonsense before I beat the truth out of you," he said.

"I'm looking for Tenora. I heard she split up with Dan."

"What do you want with Tenora?" he asked.

"That's between me and her."

"Not when you break into my place it's not. What do you want with her?"

"I have a friend who's looking to hire a law student. I thought she might be interested."

"You came here to offer Tenora a job?" he asked.

"Yeah." I looked him straight in the eye, selling the bluff as best I could.

"So why did you break in? Why are you jumping off roofs?"

"Because I'm nosy. Because I'm bored. When you didn't

answer, I broke in, and then panicked when you returned."

"What did you see?" he asked.

"Other than your reading material?"

"Yeah, other than that."

"Nothing out of the ordinary for a warehouse. Some crates."

"You look inside those crates?" he asked.

"I didn't have time. What's in them?"

Always a bad liar, he paused to think up a plausible explanation. "Oh, you missed out, man. A lot of stellar Humboldt weed," he said.

"You dealing now?" I asked.

"Me? Nah, man. One time thing. It fell in my lap."

"Too bad. Let me know. I could always use some of that Humboldt goodness," I said.

"Yeah, man. Will do. Anyway, last I heard Tenora is staying over in Oakland at her Mom's house."

"Oakland. Got it. Thanks."

"Sleeper," he said, "don't break into my place again."

"Roger," I said. "I do have one more request."

"What's that?"

I held out my hand.

"My boot?"

20

Friday, September 8th, 6 p.m.

As I walked up 6th Street toward Market, my heart still racing, I thought about the H.L. Mencken quote, "No one ever went broke underestimating the intelligence of the American public." I don't know jack about business, but I knew the only reason all my bones were still intact was because I hadn't overestimated Janks's intelligence; his prodigious stupidity had saved me from his colossal wrath.

I also knew that Janks's mental limitations weren't going to help him in the deeper waters he now inhabited. You make a mistake running guns, you wind up in jail or dead. There was no in between.

One of my life's credos is that whenever there's bad news, the best time to deliver it is never. But since I was getting paid for this bit of bad news, I headed toward Wethersby's office to brief him on what I'd learned. Wethersby wouldn't be happy there was someone out there selling guns to the Peoples Temple who could lead the government, however indirectly, back to him. Though I was a little nervous to give him this unfortunate piece of information, I leaned on another of my life's credos: if it's not my problem, then fuck it.

I was in no real rush to reach his office in the Bank of America building. He didn't seem the type to clock out at five o'clock sharp. After a pit stop at the Sutter Gutter, it was pushing six by the time I arrived at 555 California Street. All the professionals were leaving in their suits and ties. I was in my uniform, as well: pea coat, Levi's, and a knit cap. The lone change to my appearance in the past year was the short hippie ponytail I'd cut off to allow my stringy brown hair to fall just over my collar.

The elevator opened on the fiftieth floor to an art museum disguised as a law firm. The receptionist at Wethersby's firm didn't leave at 5 o'clock, either. By her model's appearance, I'd say she'd be leaving much later for a hotel with one of the partners. She gave me a pleasant, nonjudgmental once-over.

"May I help you?" she asked.

"Yes, I'm here to see Bill Wethersby."

"Your name?"

"Hayes."

After a few back-and-forths with another secretary, I was told Wethersby would see me in fifteen minutes. I used the time to brush up on my portfolio in *The Wall Street Journal* lying on the coffee table. Damn, still zero.

Wethersby came out to greet me. The look on the receptionist's face told me that this wasn't normal protocol. As usual, Wethersby was put together in a gray pinstripe suit and pink tie. I normally attribute an obsession with style in men to a shallowness of mind. For Wethersby, though, it added another layer to his considerable substance.

Back in his corner office, he directed me to a comfortable sitting area with a sweeping view of the bay, the two bridges symmetrically framing Alcatraz.

"Can I get you something," he asked. "A scotch and water?"

"You can skip the water," I replied.

"Of course." He poured a tall scotch from a clear decanter and handed it to me. He poured another, shorter one for himself.

"So I dug around for you," I began without prompting. "It's mostly good news."

"Mostly? Sounds like being kind of pregnant," he said.

"Well, the ones you're most worried about, I'm pretty sure they aren't involved." I don't know why I spoke like a Mafia Don. It's not as if saying the words New World Liberation Front was a crime.

"Okay," he replied. "That's good. But..."

"But there is another guy that laundered money through Phil who's involved, but he's as small time as you can get. I don't think there's any way anyone would connect him to you."

"What's his name?" Wethersby asked.

I paused to think whether I wanted to give up Janks's name or not. I knew that Wethersby had employed unsavory methods in the past to quiet people he viewed as threats. One reason Hammersmith reviled Wethersby so intensely was because Wethersby had won a high profile court case against the D.A.'s office by blackmailing Hammersmith's former boss over his closeted homosexuality. On the other hand, I didn't give two goddamns about Janks.

"Curtis Janko. He's an ex-hippie who's convinced himself he's a radical in order to justify his criminal activity," I said.

"You don't think he's a threat?"

"I think you're fine. Even if he gets picked up, I don't

think anyone would confuse him for a money launderer. His whole operation is this crummy little warehouse on Seventh and Harrison that I infiltrated by flicking a thin windowpane with my finger. His setup is not what I would term sophisticated."

He swirled his scotch in his glass. "Thanks, Mr. Hayes." He reached in his pocket and pulled out a crisp $100 bill. "I appreciate your help."

"Let me know if you need any more of this kind of assistance," I said, pocketing the money.

"I will."

"Oh, I almost forgot. One more thing," I said.

"Yes?"

"You have to hire a law student to work here part time."

"I do?" he asked.

"It was part of the negotiations for obtaining the information. It couldn't be avoided." While I was covering my tracks with Janks, I might as well help Tenora out in the process.

"You should have cleared it with me first," he said.

"Don't worry," I replied. "You'll be working for her at some point. Trust me." I wrote Tenora's name and number on a piece of paper. "And she'll bring some much needed color to this office."

Wethersby looked at her name. "Tenora?" he asked.

"Just give her a call and interview her. You'll be impressed."

He nodded his assent and I let myself out. When I reached the reception area, the secretary gathered her things and was escorted out by a man thirty years her senior.

Ah, the perks of partnership.

21

Friday, September 8ᵗʰ, 8 p.m.

I spent the hundred-dollar bonus the way it should be spent, quickly. I ordered a Plymouth martini and a steak at Sam's and settled in for a night of high-class gastronomy. Perched down the bar was San Francisco's favorite columnist, Herb Caen, imbibing his beloved Vitamin V. Caen was one of the worst Jim Jones apologists in town. Even after the *New West* article was published, Caen continued championing the Temple, writing that Jones was "...a target of a cease-less media barrage," and that he was, "...doing the Lord's work in Guyana."

My appetite ruined by Caen, I returned to my apartment to listen to a new stack of records from the library while I waited for Lori. A year ago, I was in a funk over the state of music. Rock was toothless and Disco and Punk, while decent side dishes, weren't worthy entrées. On some level, this dearth of good music made me happy; complaining about bad songs, for me, is almost as much fun as enjoying the good stuff.

Now, not only was I not hating anything, I was loving

everything. So much so, I worried I'd lost my edge. Punk had rubbed off on Elvis Costello, the Talking Heads, Blondie, and The Clash with spectacular results. I also knew the Disco era was almost over because I was finally on board, singing along with "*Got To Be Real*," "*Last Dance*," and "*Boogie Oogie Oogie*" whenever they played on KDIA.

While listening to Bob Seger sing "*We've Got Tonight*," I found myself looking forward to Lori's arrival. I knew I shouldn't be. That little voice inside my head was warning me not to become too attached, that addicts don't do anything halfway, and that sooner or later she would either slip back into her old ways, or even worse, demand a serious commitment from me.

I blame Seger for my confusion. You try thinking rationally while Bob pleads to some dumb bimbo to "let's make it last, let's find a way," when the name of the song was "*We've Got Tonight*."

At 9:50, the buzzer rang. A little early for Lori. Must have been a slow night at the Triangle. I cracked the door, turned up the stereo, closed my eyes, and started singing along with the Silver Bullet Band, "I know it's late. I know you're weary. I know your plans—"

"Sleeper?" a voice that wasn't Lori's interrupted my performance. I opened my eyes and saw Andre, Billy Newman's 14-year-old gopher, standing in my doorway.

"Andre? What's going on?" I asked.

"Billy wants to see you."

"Now? About what?"

"I don't know. Billy said to come down. It's an emergency." He looked at the half joint in the ashtray. "He said he doesn't care if you've been drinking, or whatever." Billy the trainer, always anticipating the angles.

"Okay," I said.

The T.L. was as loud as Andre was quiet on the walk back to Newman's. All the hustlers, pushers, and working girls were on full display, hooting and approaching us, until, recognizing our familiar faces, backing away.

The gym was dark from the outside. I opened the door and saw a sliver of light in Billy's office, where he and Alfredo sat in silence. Billy was twisting a rubber band into a cat's cradle while Alfredo reclined his head, eyes closed. Billy gave me a quick look of frustration.

"Thanks, Andre. You can go." Billy slipped him a dollar bill. "Go ahead, Fredo, tell Sleeper what you told me."

"The cops picked me up last week," Alfredo started, his eyes still closed, his head still reclined.

"What for?" I asked.

"They think I killed some girl."

I looked at Billy, who shrugged. "Why do they think that?" I asked.

"Fuck if I know, man. Said they had some evidence."

"Who was the girl?"

"Some hooker."

The walls inched closer together. I knew it was *possible* that he was talking about a hooker other than Cindy. I also knew I was kidding myself. The entropy of life, having left me alone for a while, was swirling again, colliding my worlds in the process. When worlds collide, only one thing is certain: things break.

"Was her name Cindy?" I asked.

"I don't know her name, man. Could be Cindy. Yeah, that was it. Cindy. How did you know?"

"Lucky guess," I said.

"They say I strangled her," Alfredo said.

"That's why he hasn't been training right," Billy added.

"Does Ricky know?" I asked.

"Nah. He'll kick my ass," Alfredo said.

"Not if you didn't do it," I said.

"Somehow he'll make it into my fault. You know how weird he is about sex. He already thinks I've got a problem."

"I remember that night," I said. "I was here with you. You were with Nancy. Remember, I forgot my racing form?"

"He remembers," Billy answered for him. "That's why I called you. You think you can go tell the cops you were here? You know, to confirm his alibi?"

"Why not get Nancy to do it?"

"Her husband wouldn't be too happy about that," Billy said.

"Gotcha. No problem," I said. "Whatever you need."

Billy handed me a card. "That's the cop who took him in. I guess you should talk to him," Billy said.

I looked at the card and laughed. Worlds weren't colliding; they were exploding.

"What's so funny?" Billy asked.

"Captain Stezak and I have a history."

"Good," Billy replied, not picking up on the irony. "And I got more bad news. *Some Romance* got second. Paid nineteen-fifty, too, the sonofabitch."

Just as there was no point in telling Billy he should have made a place bet, I was sure there'd be no point in telling Stezak that Alfredo was innocent. They both had their reasons for believing what they did, and neither based them on logic.

Captain Walt Stezak. *How was I supposed to approach that cocksucker?* The last I heard, from an authority no less than the FBI, he was trying to knock me off. Now I was supposed to go ask him for a favor? Stezak wasn't the forgiving or the forgetting type. The most bone-chilling example of this was his wife "committing suicide" with his service revolver after he discovered her sleeping around.

Lori wasn't in a forgiving mood, either. Under my door was a note that read, "Fool me once, shame on you. Fool me twice, shame on me. There won't be a third time." Damnit. I'd stood her up, again. Maybe when she found out the reason was related to Cindy's death she'd understand.

I called Hammersmith to see if he'd heard anything new about the case. "You guys got anything on the Triangle murder?" I asked.

"I haven't heard anything," he mumbled. I must have woken him up. "We're not consulted on every detail. Why? You hearing anything?"

"Sort of. Stezak likes a friend of mine for it," I said.

"Why is Stezak nosing around? This is homicide's case. Who does he like for it, George?"

"No. But what about George, he still the main suspect?"

"As far as I know."

"What's the motive supposed to be?" I asked, fishing to see if he'd heard anything about Cindy cooperating with the Justice Department.

"Motive? That's cop show crap. She's a hooker. He's the last john who saw her alive. That's enough."

"Thanks for the tutorial. It won't be much help for my meeting with Stezak tomorrow."

"Why do you have to meet with him?"

"Because I'm the alibi for my friend."

"Oh man, that ought to be a fun reunion, you and Stezak," he laughed.

"You want to come?"

"Nah. Three ain't company unless Suzanne Somers is involved." He chuckled at his typically stale attempt at humor.

"Guess that makes you Janet," I said.

"Yeah." He sniggered so hard he couldn't get the punchline out. "Then that makes you Mr. Fucking Rop—"

I hung up on him before he could finish. A new low, outwitted by Hammersmith. Then I chuckled, too.

Mr. Fucking Roper.

22

Monday, September 11th, 10 a.m.

I boiled some water for my Folgers after my third straight night of spotty sleep and put on a pair of brown cords, a maroon sweatshirt, and brown workboots. Over the weekend, I'd steadied myself for my meeting with Stezak by listening to another of my library withdrawals, Emmylou's *Quarter Moon in a Ten Cent Town*.

Not even Emmylou could take my mind off Stezak. The last man I ever feared was my father. After surviving his religious fire and brimstone—it's tough to threaten any more than eternal damnation—every other bully I encountered was an amateur.

It was different with Stezak. Maybe because I viewed him more as reptilian than human. Throw me into the swamps of Florida and I'd be damn scared of alligators. It was the same with Stezak. The Tenderloin was his natural habitat and he was the undisputed king.

I knocked on Nelson's door on the way out. He was sitting on his couch, reading the paper, still comatose.

"Good news," I said. "We hit a race at Bay Meadows yesterday. Paid nine to one to place. We're up to four hundred and twenty now."

"Cool. I made twenty yesterday selling weed. Take this." He handed me ten dollars.

"Only one thousand seven hundred and forty dollars to go," I said.

"The journey of a thousand miles…" he started.

"…begins with a quarter horse race at Bay Meadows," I finished.

As I left he turned on the radio, snapping along to The O'Jays's "*Use Ta Be My Girl.*" It was the first crack I'd seen in the ice of his post-robbery funk.

I pulled my brown knit cap tight over my ears as I walked north through the Stockton tunnel into Chinatown, where the fog still lingered.

"Is Captain Stezak available?" I asked the duty officer at Central Station.

"Is he expecting you?"

"Sort of," I replied.

He dialed the phone, perking up a bit after relaying my name to Stezak. He repeated it while giving me a more focused once over, like he was picking out a pork chop from the butcher.

"Yeah, that about describes him," he said, hanging up.

A flattering portrait was painted, I'm sure.

Stezak appeared in the doorway behind the desk. He cocked his head to the side and motioned to me with his index finger. I followed him down the dingy hall into his small, windowless office. His walls were covered with plaques ranging from P.A.L. softball championships to Mayoral and Presidential commendations, with no thought or hierarchy to their arrangement.

He nodded at the chair in front of his desk, still no words spoken between us. He continued staring, then nodded his head again, my cue to talk.

"I'm here about Alfredo Flores." His eyes widened just enough that I knew I'd caught him off guard. "I was with him the night Cindy Teague was murdered."

He shrugged his shoulders.

"I know you're looking at him for the murder," I continued. "I'm telling you I was with him. It wasn't Alfredo."

No response. He grimaced and scratched his lizard-like face. "Sleeper Hayes," he said. "Sleeper, goddamn, moron, alcoholic Hayes."

"That's not technically my middle name but..."

"Shut up," he snapped. "I'm not done. You are one upside down idiot, you know that?"

"That would explain some things about my life."

"I said, shut up. In fact, I should call you Wrong Way Hayes. I told you last year that Phil Matthews killed himself and you didn't believe me. Now you know I wasn't lying. Yet you ignored my warning and wound up making a fool of yourself. More important, you tried to make a fool of me. I don't like being made a fool of by residents of my own district. Of all the things people expect of me, the one thing I should be able to deliver is control over my territory."

"There's a job opening at the Kremlin that would be perfect for you," I said.

"Keep up the sarcasm. It's gotten you this far in life."

"Look." I backed off. "I wasn't trying to make a fool of you then and I'm not now. I'm trying to keep you from looking like one."

Stezak pulled out one of his trademark cigars from his shirt pocket and started chewing on it. "The problem is, Wrong Way," he said. "We have evidence linking Flores to the crime. So despite your plea, Flores is our man until we say he isn't."

"What kind of evidence?" I asked.

"You don't expect me to share that with you, do you?"

"I guess I did."

"Well, you're probably drunk, so I can't blame you." He lit his stogie with a smug, self-satisfied flourish. "Bring me another suspect and we'll look at him, too. That's the best offer I can make."

It was more than I expected.

I thought about George and the fact that Cindy was co-operating with Justice. I knew what Stezak would do with that information. Guilty or not, he would use it to leverage George somehow. Money, a favor, something.

"Anyone?" he repeated.

"So my word means nothing to you?" I asked.

"Not one damn cent."

About what my life was worth to him, as well.

"Fine. George Urbancyck," I said.

"Not buying," he replied.

"Why not?"

"Everyone knows he loved that girl."

"Maybe she didn't love him so much," I said.

"Why would you say that?"

"I think she could have been ratting him out to the Justice Department."

He started puffing on that cigar like he was sending smoke signals to a neighboring tribe. I had his attention.

"And you think George found out?" he asked. The good thing about cops like Stezak is you don't have to connect all the crooked dots for them.

"I don't know," I said. "I only know Alfredo didn't do it."

"So Urbancyck, huh?" I saw him assessing the situation, figuring out the best way to take advantage of it. "Okay. Thanks."

"So you'll lay off Alfredo?"

"While I run this George thing down, yeah. After that, we'll see."

I walked out into the now fogless sky, my job done. Stezak had taken the bait. Now it was up to George to fend for himself. At least it would be a fair fight between two heavyweights.

I hauled it back to a bustling Newman's. Don Stewart's number one was sparring with a few of Pete Castillo's boys. Alfredo was in the bleachers talking to some girl who looked like Farrah Fawcett dipped in caramel.

Just for a day, I thought.

Ricky was alone with Billy in his office.

"Is this a good time?" I asked, unsure if Ricky knew what was happening with Alfredo.

"Come on in, Sleeper," Billy said. "Ricky's up to speed. You talk to that cop friend of yours?"

"Yeah. I should have made it clear last night that the cop and I aren't friends."

"No?" Billy asked.

"No. In fact, it's the opposite. But I went anyway and told him that I was with Alfredo the night of the murder. He didn't care. Says they got evidence linking him to the crime."

"What evidence?" Ricky asked.

"Wouldn't say. All he said was bring him a suspect better than Alfredo and he'd take a look."

"Isn't that his job?" Billy asked.

"Not Stezak's," I said. "His job is to throw someone in jail, innocent or guilty, and if he can make a buck in the process, even better. I threw him a name, anyway."

"Who?" Ricky asked.

"Doesn't matter. It won't solve our problem, but it will keep him busy until the fight."

"What do I tell Alfredo if it doesn't?" Ricky asked.

Everyone was quiet, and, for some damn reason, looking at me for an answer. "Lie to him." They stared at me like I'd asked someone to shoot the president. "I'm serious. We all know he didn't do it. Tell him the cops have backed off. Calm him down. In the meantime, let me see what I can find out."

"That's your plan?" Billy asked.

"You got a better one?"

23

Saturday, September 16th, 4 p.m.

Five days later, it was fight night. Alfredo had trained flaw-lessly since being unburdened of the specter of Stezak, and was ready to take his next step to greatness at the San Carlos Circle Star Theater.

"No more quarter horse bets," Dmitri barked as soon as I stepped through the Acropolis's door to bet on Alfredo for Nelson's burgeoning album fund.

"I told you to lay some of it off."

"And hell if I didn't. Satterfield isn't very happy with you, either." Dmitri chuckled. Marvin Satterfield was another Tenderloin bookie whom Dmitri must have split the bet with.

"I want down on Alfredo tonight," I replied.

"Who doesn't? The line is minus one thousand and there's a two hundred dollar max."

That was 1-10 odds. For every $10 bet, you only win $1 back.

That's a gift.

"That's a rip-off," I said.

"That's a lay-up and you know it," Dmitri replied. "Better

not complain too much. You might not have many alternatives soon." He was referring to the recent citywide sweep that the IRS did of twelve gambling operations. Even the damn taxman was snooping around the city now.

"Or you could be the next to get cuffed," I said. "Fine. I'll take two hundred on Alfredo."

"I'll pay you fifteen now not to bet," Dmitri said.

"Eighteen and it's a deal."

"You're down for two hundred," Dmitri replied. "Maybe Alfredo will slip and knock himself out."

"Seventeen?"

"Don't push your luck," he said.

"I wouldn't dare. It's all I got."

Hammersmith and I drove his beat-up Chevy Nova down 101 through rush hour traffic. I rummaged through his eight tracks on the passenger side floorboard. Hammersmith's taste in music was straight rock, straight crap. The more bombastic, the more he liked it. Instead of choosing between Foreigner, Rush, or Styx I opted for the radio.

"Ten dollar bet on who KYA is playing, the Bee Gees or Abba? Anything from *Grease* is a push," I proposed.

"You're on. Definitely ABBA," Hammersmith replied.

I hit his preset button. "Night Fever" was cranking.

"Thank you for your donating to the Nelson LP recovery fund," I said. "When are you gonna get a cassette deck anyway?"

"You think they'll replace eight tracks?"

"Yeah. I think."

"Given your business acumen, which has taken you all the way to the bowels of the Tenderloin, I hope you don't mind if I ignore your advice," he said.

"Fine. Don't believe me. But you should sell these all back to Bill before they're worth nothing." I took a shot of Johnnie from my flask.

"Careful with that," Hammersmith said. "I wouldn't want you to stain the leather."

"This is pleather, not leather, and it doesn't stain," I said. "Hey, did I tell you who Justice's latest suspect in Cindy's murder is?"

"Who's that?"

"You're looking at him," I said.

"Seriously?"

"So they say. I think they want to jam up George and they thought I'd roll."

"You're probably right. They counted on Buster rolling and he didn't. Now they're on to Plan B. Maybe Plan Z if they're down to you." Hammersmith laughed at his zinger.

"The thing is, I'd give them something if I had it," I said. "I want Stezak off Alfredo's back for good. Is anyone looking into the Peoples Temple angle?"

"The Angels?"

"Yeah."

"Nobody is looking into that," Hammersmith said.

"Why not?"

"Well, between the Golden Dragon case, the parking meter scandal, and the Zebra Murders appeal, we don't have a lot of manpower right now to investigate all your crazy theories."

"They should. They're the only plausible suspects."

"You mean except for George and Alfredo."

"Yeah, except them," I said.

"Any other brilliant suggestions?" he asked.

"Yeah. Double or nothing that Alfredo wins in less than three rounds."

"I'll take two," Hammersmith said.

"I'll take one," I said.

"You're on."

The Circle Star was a theater-in-the-round with a rotating stage. Nearly every major comedian and R&B act had played there since it started featuring concerts in 1971. For music, the rotating stage was awkward and distracting. For boxing, when it was immobile, it was perfect. Almost every one of the 3,000 seats, even the cheap ones, had a clear view. Most fight nights, the place was half-filled; tonight, for Alfredo, the place was packed.

The preliminary fights were either mismatches or glorified sparring sessions. It wasn't until Golden Gloves heavyweight champ Vinnie Hines KO'd "Smooth" Larry Barber in the 5th round of the penultimate fight that we watched our first real bout of the night.

At last, it was Alfredo's turn. Despite having top billing, he entered the ring before his opponent. If he noticed the focus of 3,000 people on him, I couldn't tell. Surrounding him were Ricky, Billy, and his cut man, Slops. Alfredo wore a black and gold robe with a lizard on the back. I'd have to have a talk with him about his choice of mascot later.

Alfredo looked relaxed, like he was walking down Market Street on a Saturday night. He stepped inside the ropes, shadow boxed, danced, and hammed it up for the crowd. He flashed a big smile and winked to fans in the front row before Ricky corralled him to give him his instructions.

Meanwhile, his opponent, Hector Martinez, entered the

ring unnoticed. Though the same 147 pounds as Alfredo, he looked tiny by comparison. This perception was due to how Alfredo carried his weight. Alfredo was taller than the average welterweight and most of his girth was in his upper body. The large boxing shorts helped hide his spindly legs. Billy thought Alfredo would ultimately fill out his frame and box as a middleweight.

They went to their corners and Ricky jammed his finger into Alfredo's chest, imploring him to get serious. Alfredo continued smiling.

"He looks a little too relaxed, don't you think?" Hammersmith asked me.

"I've seen this before. As soon as the bell rings, he'll snap into focus." Alfredo didn't need to psyche himself into being a boxer; he was one.

The bell rang and the switch inside Alfredo flipped. He pounced on Hector, springing halfway across the ring before Hector could even get his hands up. Hector's defense was to run away from him. Unfortunately for Hector, Alfredo was not only stronger than him, but faster. Alfredo caught him in two strides and connected with a ferocious right hook. Through his protective stance, Hector looked at Alfredo like he was looking at an alien. He tried to circle the ring a few times to get some breathing room, but Alfredo wouldn't let him.

Hector, realizing there was no place to run, stopped and went toe-to-toe with him. Three Alfredo uppercuts later, it was over. Alfredo bowed in every direction, then hugged Hector after his trainer had helped him off the canvas.

Hammersmith looked at me like he'd seen Big Foot.

"I wish they charged us by the minute," he said. "We'd

have saved a lot of money."

"Boxers and hookers," I replied, "the better they are at their job, the quicker the fun is over."

24

Sunday, September 17ᵗʰ, 12 a.m.

Hammersmith dropped me off at the Triangle. The fight had kick-started my animal instincts and I wanted to see how primal Lori was feeling, assuming she'd forgiven me.

Again, no Lori behind the bar.

"Where is she?" I asked Vic, accepting the glass of Johnnie he'd poured me.

"Another no-show. Frank's not happy about it."

My heart sank. I wished I didn't always assume the worst. I wished my worst assumptions weren't always right. Most of all, I wished I could quit wishing.

I finished my drink and marched to Lori's apartment. I knocked on her door. No answer. *Where was she?* Someplace else. Someplace no good.

I left Lori's in desperate need of another drink. After stopping at Donny's for a few, then a few more, I staggered home and fumbled with my keys at the front door. As I bent down and closed one eye in order to insert the key in what I swear was a swaying lock, somebody grabbed the back of my hair and slammed my face into the gate. He enjoyed it so much, he did it again.

"Who the fuck did you talk to?"

"Janks?" I moaned.

"You douchebag. Who did you talk to?"

"Stop banging my head against the door so I can concentrate." The pounding paused, but the hand remained attached to my hair. "Thank you," I continued. "Now what are you talking about?"

"The cops raided my warehouse. Knew my name. Knew about the guns. You saying it's a coincidence they busted me a few weeks after you were skulking around?"

"I didn't talk to anyone."

"Bullshit."

He spun me around and pushed me against the concrete railing on the steps, seizing my neck. My head dangled over the side and my back arched like a McDonald's sign. Yoga for degenerates. Janks squeezed my neck with both hands. I couldn't breathe, much less talk, and I was too drunk to offer any real resistance.

My vision started constricting, like a camera shutter closing. I tried to think of something profound; I wanted my last thoughts to be something memorable. Instead, all I could think of was why weren't The Kinks at least as popular as Led Zeppelin.

The pressure on my neck ceased and was replaced by the pressure of Janks's inert body on top of mine. I slid out from under him, my vision still foggy. I regained my senses and saw Nelson holding his cane like a baseball bat, waiting for Janks to make a move.

I took the cane from Nelson and poked Janks. He was alive, despite the two-inch gash on the back of his head.

I attempted my own swing at his ribs, but it landed like a jazz drummer brushing a snare drum. I tried again with the same result. Nelson grabbed the cane and guided me up to my bed.

Nobody to blame but yourself. You took Wethersby's job. It's called blood money for a reason.

25

Sunday, September 17th, 2 p.m.

I can't say for sure whether I slept at all that night or if I was dreaming. My mind raced between the fight, Janks, Lori, Cindy, George, Stezak, the FBI, the Justice Department, and Jim Jones. If it was a dream, I shuddered to think what Freud would have made of that jumble of characters.

I read about the fight in the following day's *Chronicle*, which described the final sequence as "a series of jabs, followed by two combinations, three body punches, and a right cross." I suppose that was an accurate, technical recounting of the fight. It also failed in every way to convey the magic of what I witnessed. My description of the night would go something like this:

"What if you had seen the first trickle of paint drip off Jackson Pollock's brush onto a blank canvas? What if you'd been in Picasso's studio when he initially tweaked the nose on one of his portraits? How about if you'd heard Keith Richards strum the guitar hook to "Satisfaction" in his Florida hotel room? Or been in Newport when Dylan and The Band plugged in their guitars?"

I would have added Marvin Gaye to that list, but I wouldn't want to be accused of exaggerating Alfredo's gifts.

There were finger marks on both sides of my neck and broken capillaries around my eyes. Despite the injuries Janks had inflicted on me, I agreed with him that it wasn't a coincidence the cops showed up at his warehouse so soon after I visited him. His one miscalculation was that it was Wethersby, not me, who'd dropped the dime.

My whole life had become asking people whether they'd done something illicit, illegal, or immoral, then trying to decipher the truth after their denial. I was a human polygraph machine. I had no reason to think my impending conversation with Wethersby would be any different.

I took the 45 bus over to Pacific Heights, where the Wethersbys were having a barbeque in their backyard with their neighbors, the Jentrys. The Jentrys were the same neighbors who had been held hostage by the NWLF and released after hours of supposedly brilliant negotiations by Wethersby, the actual terms of which he was still working to keep undisclosed.

The adults at the party were in separate circles of a half a dozen each, divided by gender. A few younger kids were playing steal the bases, including Wethersby's youngest boy, Kevin, and the Gentrys' son, Jeff. Miriam, his troubled adult daughter, was sitting on the deck stairs by herself, smoking a cigarette. Apart from the dour look on her face, she looked healthy, stunning even. The cliché is that looks can be deceiving. I've found that's not the case when drugs are involved. If you're using, there are visual clues, the main one being you look like hell. Miriam didn't look like hell.

I waited on the driveway until I caught Wethersby's eye. He was surprised but, as usual, unruffled. He waved me over to an empty picnic table away from the group.

"Mr. Hayes, can I offer you something?" he asked.

Not wanting to be accused of being a social climber, I got right to the point. "No thanks. The cops busted that guy's warehouse," I said.

"Oh, yes. I'm aware. How do you know?"

I pointed to the red marks on both sides of my neck. "He blames me."

"Oh."

"Better question, how do you know?" I asked.

"I should know. I'm representing him."

"You're what?" I asked.

"I'm Mr. Janko's lawyer."

That wasn't what I was expecting to hear. I was used to dealing with the transparent hustle of the Tenderloin. The game played by the likes of Wethersby, Stezak, and George required a PhD in game theory. I wasn't sure I was up to it. It was the difference between playing Old Maid and seven-card stud.

"You had him picked up, didn't you?" I asked.

"Why would I do that?" he asked, like a teacher questioning a student.

"Because that way you can control the situation. Janks can't say anything to the cops that you don't allow him to say," I said.

"I can't comment. Lawyer-client confidentiality."

"Of course not," I replied, though he had confirmed my suspicions. He was good. Most people would hope that

Janks was never busted. Wethersby, being the pro that he is, arranges for it, insuring nothing incriminating ever sees the light of day. "Miriam looks good," I said, changing the subject.

"She's doing better. Thanks. Would you like to say hi?"

"I'd better not. I don't want to drudge up any bad memories."

"That's considerate of you," he said.

"Not all of us in the T.L. are Neanderthals."

"And not all of us in Pacific Heights are Marie Antoinette," Wethersby replied.

"Fair enough," I said, shaking his hand. "Well, I'm off to eat my cake."

26

Saturday, September 23rd, 10 p.m.

"I fold," I said, for what felt like the forty-second time that night.

"Shocker," Clyde replied.

"Don't blame me. Blame Niko over there. Deal me one decent hand, would ya?"

With three regulars and two new fish at the table, it was a bad night to pull rags. On the other hand, even if I hadn't profited from the fish, they'd at least kept me from being cleaned out like I should have been long ago.

"Keh, keh," one of the newbies coughed for what also seemed like the forty-second time that night.

"Then there is Mr. Sniffles over there," I said. "Hey, next time you're sick why don't you stay home instead of infecting everyone else."

"Keh, keh," he repeated.

"And cough like a man, why don't you? You cough like a little girl. 'Keh, keh,'" I imitated him.

Everyone but Sniffles laughed. What was wrong with people?

The night went on much the same. I never got a card and Mr. Sniffles kept coughing like a pansy. I clawed my way to break-even by taking Sniffles out of his remaining chips with my one good hand that everyone else at the table saw a mile away.

"Where you headed now, Sniffles, the E.R.?" I asked.

"You're a funny guy. You should be careful," he wheezed.

"I'll be careful not to catch your cold."

"You do that," he said, and shuffled out the door.

"Who invites these guys, Niko?" I asked. "Seriously, tell Dmitri to start screening better. It's a goddamn embarrassment who you guys let into these games."

"Speaking of embarrassments," Niko replied, "how about them Niners?"

"Terrible, even with O.J.," Clyde agreed.

"Niner fans better buckle up for another bad year," I said.

"Buckle up?" Yuri asked.

"Yeah, buckle up for another bad ride."

"Where are they going?" Yuri said.

"It's a euphemism, you pinko. Another bad season."

"But they don't wear seatbelts to play football, do they?"

I threw my cards on the table and looked at Yuri, ready to explode, until I saw the slightest of smiles cross his lips.

"You bastard," I said. "You're just trying to get my goat."

"You own a goat?" Yuri said.

"Screw off, Yuri."

"You think the Yankees will hold on, Sleeper?" Clyde asked.

"It's free money," I said.

"How's that?"

"All you have to do is bet against the Red Sox. There is no stopping this collapse now." If there was anything I was

122

an expert on, it was collapses. They either toughen people or break them. Enough evidence was in to see that the Red Sox were broken. They'd been leading the Yankees by 14 1/2 games in July, but after the Yankees swept four games at Fenway, they were now tied. I'd already made two hundred betting against them for Nelson's record fund, and I planned on doubling that during the final stretch of the season.

We pushed around chips for another half hour then called it a night with no real damage done to anyone. I bet $20 on the Raiders and my man Kenny Stabler on the way out.

I inhaled the cool Tenderloin night. I wouldn't trade San Francisco weather for anywhere in the world. So what if the sun doesn't shine that much? All that does is ensure I never have to see a bunch of sweaty, fat people in bathing suits. That reminded me to add 'people who sunbathe' to my and Donny's list.

Out on the street, I lit a jet and saw Mr. Sniffles walking toward me with a handkerchief in his hand.

"Hey, that's a start," I said. "You bought a handkerchief."

He responded by pointing his handkerchief at me, and I'll be damned if a bullet didn't shoot out from under that thing, hitting me smack in the chest. Three years in the Navy, four more in the Tenderloin, and I'd never been shot. Now here I was, slumping to the ground on Mason Street, the world fading to black, done in by Mr. Fucking Sniffles.

27

Thursday, September 28th, 3 p.m.

Even if all my friends had been in my hospital room when I awoke, I wouldn't have been able to acknowledge any of them with the giant tube that was stuck down my throat. I tilted my head downward and saw my torso wrapped in bandages, a blot of red seeping through on my right side. Ten minutes later, a nurse entered the small, glue-colored room.

"Good morning, Mr. Hayes."

I grunted a response.

"Do you know where you are?"

I shook my head.

"You're at St. Francis's Hospital. Do you know why you're here?"

I nodded.

"Good. I'll call the doctor to come explain your situation. Anything else I can do for you?"

I pointed to the tube.

"The doctor will be in soon," she said.

'Soon' in hospital terms must mean something different than it does everywhere else on Earth. A few hours and naps later, a high schooler masquerading as a doctor introduced himself.

"I'm Dr. Gallo," he said. "How are you feeling, Mr. Hayes?"

I pointed at the tube, again.

"That will have to stay in for another week."

Then stop with the twenty fucking questions, already.

"You were shot in the chest, Mr. Hayes, on the far right side of your rib cage. Do you remember that?"

I nodded.

"Good. Lucky for you the shot was outside the nipples."

I gave him a confused look. *Why did this fruit care about my nipples?*

"That means it avoided any vital organs. You lost some blood, broke some ribs, and your right lung was damaged. That lung is our only real concern. We'll need to keep you here for at least another week until we can pump it back up with oxygen. After that, you'll be in considerable pain for a couple of months.

"Needless to say, you won't be running any marathons anytime soon. But in the long run, the bullet will have done much less damage to your lung than those cigarettes you smoke. Meanwhile, if you're in too much pain, you can self-medicate yourself by pressing this button. The morphine will do the rest."

After the doctor left. I pressed the morphine button like I was ringing in on *The Family Feud*. The hospital was going to lose a lot of money on me.

I was in and out of consciousness for a few days, until finally awaking one morning to Nelson holding a boom box the size of a suitcase, cranking "20th Century Man." Having

125

become an expert at conveying information with my eyes, I gave him an approving look.

"It's Donny's. He says get well soon. He also says he has some new entries for your list, whatever that is," Nelson said.

I found the pad of paper I'd requested from the nurse and wrote, *List of profound stupidity. How are you?*

"Better after hearing you got shot."

I wrote a big question mark on the pad.

"It snapped me out of my self-pity. Made me realize what a baby I was being about my record collection."

Glad I could help, I wrote.

Nelson did look better. His complexion had gone from a dull oatmeal to a shiny pecan, his cardigan and cords looked recently laundered, his afro recently picked.

He pulled out the sports page and smiled at me. Nelson not being a sports fan, I didn't understand the implication.

"Wanna make a bet?" he asked.

More than anything in the world, I wrote.

I looked over the gambling lines. There was one silver lining to being shot: it had saved me money betting against the Red Sox. Boston had made a remarkable comeback, winning their last eight games, to tie the division. They were playing the Yankees today in a one-game playoff at Fenway. I pointed a finger at the Yankees. In order for Red Sox fans to suffer the most pain, and true suffering is the essence of sports fandom, the Yankees had to win.

Nelson phoned in the bet to Dmitri, then stayed with me the rest of the day, listening to the game on the radio. The Yankees won, and our kitty was now up to a thousand dollars. Nelson was more encouraged than I was. I'd won a lot of bets in a row, and we were still a grand away from our goal.

A cold streak was coming sooner or later.

The next morning I hit my emotional breaking point. The tube in my mouth was unbearable, and I was tired of consuming and disposing all of my food through bags. I was in no mood for the three visitors who then walked through the door. It was Hackett from the Justice Department and his two Village People, now dressed in ill-fitting suits.

"Does that tube come out?" the boss asked.

I shook my head.

He stared at the Village People.

"How were we supposed to know?" big giant answered Hackett.

"Because it's your job?" Hackett replied. I waved the notepad in the air. "Okay, good," he said. "I stopped by to see if this shooting made you change your mind about George Urbancyck."

No. Why would it? I wrote.

"You might want to reconsider that opinion." He tossed a manila folder onto my chest. "That the guy who shot you?"

I pulled a mug shot out of the folder. There he was, Mr. Sniffles.

I nodded.

"His name is Charlie Christano. Charlie Christ to the Feds. He's a freelance button man. Does work for the mob, but he's not too particular about his clients."

I stared at the photo. Though he looked different in the mug shot—no glasses, long hair, tanned—there was no doubt it was Sniffles. I noted the county of imprisonment, Dade County, Florida. Explained the tan, at least. I'd read

Sniffles' poker hands correctly, but man had I misread him.

"Don't be thick," Hackett continued. "You have to know that the mob and the unions share a bed. Charlie did work for the unions back east until the heat got too hot, so he moved his operation out west. *Now* is there anything you want to tell us about George?"

I turned away from him.

"Alright, your choice." He picked up the picture and returned it to the folder. "Your loyalty is misplaced, Mr. Hayes."

As they were leaving, the little giant piped up, "Next time we have this conversation, it'll be in the morgue."

Hackett rolled his eyes, berating him as they left.

Ah, George. I wondered what the Shakespeare quotation was for "You have some fucking explaining to do."

The following day, the tube came out.

"Here, drink some water," Dr. Gallo said. "As soon as you can stand, eat, and go to the bathroom without any help, you can go home."

"That's it?" I croaked.

"That's it," he said. "But I think you'll find the last requirement isn't as easy as you remember. I'm writing you a prescription for Vicodin. Please use these pills the way they're intended, to alleviate pain, not to enhance pleasure."

"What's the difference?" I said.

"Medically, there's a difference. You also need to know that your lung is in a vulnerable state. If you keep smoking, it might never recover."

"How about weed?" I asked.

"Same."

The nurse knocked on the door. "Visitors okay?"

"I'm all done," the doctor said, passing my visitor on his way out.

"You dumb bastard," Hammersmith said. "You went and popped off to the wrong guy, didn't you?"

"Something like that."

"So when are you out?" he asked.

"As soon as I can walk, eat, and take a leak by myself."

"You couldn't do those things *before* you were shot," he said.

"I see you haven't lost your razor-sharp wit."

"Well, I didn't come down here solely to bust your balls. I talked to the lead investigators on Cindy's murder in homicide. Alfredo isn't even on their radar. Stezak is a lone wolf on that."

"What's Stezak's angle?" I asked.

"I don't know, but there has to be one. You sure you don't want to tell anyone about Cindy meeting with the Justice Department?"

"Let me think about it," I said. In light of the Charlie Christano connection, I had to talk with George one more time, face-to-face, before I told the authorities.

"Drinks when you're ready?" Hammersmith asked.

"I was born ready."

"In that case..." Hammersmith pulled a pint of Johnnie out of his pocket and slid it under my blanket. He patted my shoulder, winked, and walked out like he'd performed the greatest act of bravery in the history of the world, a fact I wouldn't dispute.

28

Twenty-four hours later—the bathroom requirement was indeed a little tricky—I gingerly dressed myself to leave the hospital. It was a drawn-out process, having to rest once after a good ten-minute struggle putting on my shirt, and again after threading my right leg through my pants. There was no rush. Nelson, my escort, had no place to be.

Between me needing to rest every half block and Nelson hobbling along with his cane, the ten minute walk from the hospital took over an hour. Getting shot was the easy part; it's the recovery that's a bitch.

We arrived at my apartment to find the door cracked a few inches. We exchanged confused looks. Nelson eased it open with his cane, exposing a tied and gagged Lady Ellinger seated on my recliner.

Nelson and I limped over together and untied her.

"That bitch!" Lady screamed, as soon as I pulled the sock from her mouth.

"What happened?" Nelson asked.

"I caught some crazy bitch breaking into Sleeper's apart-

130

ment. She pushed me inside and tied me up."

"How long have you been here?" I asked.

"About an hour."

"Are you okay?" Nelson asked.

"Don't patronize me. Of course I am."

"What did she want?" I asked, handing her a glass of water.

"How should I know, you idiot? Look around."

I did as she commanded. The room was ransacked. Thoroughly. Professionally.

"She took a box with a bunch of files in it," Lady continued.

"Red ones?"

"Yes."

"What did she look like?" I asked, though I already knew the answer.

"Ugly little wench. Gray hair. Looked like a boy. Face like a horse."

"Or a wolf?" I asked.

"That, too."

"I'm sorry, Lady," I said, helping her up. "No need to worry. I know who she was and she got what she was after. She won't be back again."

"Oh, I hope she comes back," said Lady. "I'll beat her little bony ass if I ever see her again."

Nelson and I both chuckled at Lady's full-blooded spirit.

"Here, let me take you upstairs," Nelson offered.

"Thank you, Nelson," Lady replied. "You were always the gentleman of this duo." She gave me a disapproving look.

"Goodbye, Lady," I replied, appropriately chastened.

I hadn't lied to Lady, though. There was no reason for her to be worried about another visit from the Temple's operative. I wish I could say the same for myself. I was plenty troubled by the fact that the Temple had somehow found out not only my name, but also where I lived.

29

Monday, October 9th, 4 p.m.

I spent the rest of the weekend living the Tenderloin version of "It's a Wonderful Life." Martha Samadi, from the A.M. Market, and Lady Ellinger brought me food; Hammersmith brought me scotch; and Nelson, knowing the doctor's ban on smoking, brought me a pan of pot brownies. He also went to the library and brought me some music and books. All my angels earned their wings.

The one person absent was Lori, something Nelson addressed one night while we listened to "Good Luck Charm" by the Ohio Players.

"You know Lori is using again, right?"

"That started before the shooting," I said. "How do you know?"

"She's working down at the Square Chair now."

"Makes sense. Similar type of place to the Triangle," I said.

"Umm, Sleeper?"

"Huh?"

"She ain't bartending there," Nelson said.

"Then what's she do—"

133

Oh, that.

Nelson confirmed my suspicion with an empathetic nod.

Oh.

That.

The news about Lori hooking was as difficult to overcome as the bullet wound. I knew Lori had fallen off the wagon. I didn't know she had fallen this fast or this far.

What the hell? Had I misjudged Lori's resolve? Were there any red flags I'd missed? If I hadn't been in the hospital, could I have stopped the slide? Maybe it wasn't too late to help, I thought, though I wasn't sanguine about that possibility. I've found it's up to each addict to decide when enough is enough. Despite these misgivings, and my poor physical condition, I headed to the Chair to check out Lori's situation for myself.

The Square Chair was starker than the Triangle. More sinister. Its lights were dimmed for anonymity, not atmosphere. I held out hope that Nelson's information about Lori was faulty until I walked in and saw her sitting alone at a back table. The pain in my lung merged with an ache I was feeling in another nearby body organ.

Other than the heavy makeup, Lori wasn't dressed like a whore. At first I thought she was shaking at the sight of me, then I realized it was because she was jonesing.

"Hi, Lori." I sat down across from her.

"Sleeper," she said. Her eyes darted around the room. "What are you doing here?"

"I came here to ask you the same question." She'd lost fifteen pounds and her skin and hair were drained of color.

"You shouldn't be here unless you want a date," she said.

"A date, as in pay you?" I asked.

"Sal will be back soon. You gotta go."

"Who's that, your pimp?"

Even in her manic state, that word cut her deep. "Leave me alone."

"You want H? I'll get you H. Just walk out of here with me," I said.

"You have some heroin?"

"Yes," I lied. "Come with me. It's back in my apartment."

She scanned the room again. "Don't lie to me," she said. "I need it bad."

"I'm not lying," I said.

I heard the door close behind me. Lori, recognizing whoever walked in, put down her purse.

"Going somewhere?" a twitchy, bowlegged Italian runt asked us.

"No place, Sal," Lori responded. "We're only talking."

"This ain't the place for conversation, buddy," Sal said to me. "Pay up or take a walk."

"Do you want to go with me?" I asked Lori.

"You don't ask her," he said.

"Lori, let's walk out of here right now."

"What's this asshole talking about, Lori? You two aren't going anywhere." Sal opened his jacket and displayed a hunting knife hanging from his belt. "But you are," he continued, jerking me from the table. I seized up, the pain from my lung shooting through my entire body. "What's wrong with you?" he asked.

"Nothing," I winced.

"Then get the fuck out of here." He turned his back to the bar and took the blade from its case. "If you think I won't

135

do it, ask her," he said.

I looked at Lori for direction.

"Leave me alone, mister," she said, rubbing her stomach.

"You heard her," Sal followed up. "Get out."

"I'm leaving," I said. "But we'll be seeing each other again."

"Anytime, buddy," he replied, and held up the knife, its blade catching the one ray of light shooting out from behind the bar.

Needing to wash the grime from the Square off of me, I hobbled straight to Newman's. I wanted to see young, active, healthy people. I wanted to see Alfredo.

On my way to the gym, a homeless man in a Navy pea coat much like mine approached me on the street asking for change. I reached in my pocket and gave him what I had, fifteen cents.

The faded name on his jacket, Branson, was the same as a guy I served with 15 years ago. I examined him more closely. It was him. It didn't take a doctor to diagnose his condition: drugs, hard ones. His head, eyes, and feet all twitched from side to side, and his tan-looking skin was really a thin film of dirt. If he returned my stare all day he wouldn't have recognized me. He must have reenlisted and wound up deep in Vietnam. I don't know what happened over there, but I'd seen enough guys come back like Archie Branson to know that it was something the rest of us would never understand by reading *Time*.

Goddamn life. Keeps going on.

Archie made me consider the Tenderloin. The T.L. was always the place where San Francisco's outcasts gathered. Criminals, ex-cons, alcoholics, hookers, castoffs, hard-luck cases, and straight-up weirdos. These people were my people. People with unfixable flaws who, more often than not, lose whatever battles they're fighting.

But the T.L. wasn't only a wasteland of losers. It was also a place to have some fun. The neon lights of the Tenderloin's hotels and bars were as recognizable to locals as the Golden Gate Bridge. The Black Hawk Lounge on Hyde and Turk used to host all the jazz greats, from Billie Holiday to Johnny Mathis to Charlie Parker; Polo's and Original Joe's still served food with style; and whatever your sexual proclivities and predilections, the Tenderloin had a bar for you.

Lately, though, the T.L. was becoming a touch more desperate, a bit more violent. Every year a few more homeless panhandled, a few more murders occurred, and a few more dope fiends overdosed. The fun was slowly seeping out, and more and more I found myself looking over my shoulder when I heard footsteps behind me late at night.

I entered Newman's and Billy spotted me from his perch on the bleachers. "Hey, look what the cat dragged in! How you feeling?" he asked.

"Like I went fifteen rounds with Frazier." I shook his hand and sat down. "Speaking of heavyweights, why's Alfredo sparring with one?"

We looked at the ring, where Alfredo was trading punches with a guy that looked twenty pounds heavier than Alfredo. "Ricky's stepping up the training for the Ward fight in three weeks," Billy replied. "He wants to find out if Alfredo can take a punch."

"Why?"

"Because nobody has been able to land a good one on him during a fight. His jaw is his only question mark and

Ricky wants to answer that question before he steps in the ring again. Virgil may be dumb and slow, but he has a heavy right cross."

"Isn't there a better way to test for that?" I asked.

"He's conditioning Alfredo's chin by strengthening his neck. But the only way to know whether someone can take a punch is to get punched."

"You're all a bunch of masochists," I said.

"Says the guy who got shot."

"Not by choice," I said. "Stezak back hawking Alfredo?"

"Nope."

"Good." My diversion with Stezak was still working. And the news about Sniffles the shooter being mobbed up made me feel less guilty about throwing him George's name. It also reminded me that I had forgotten something important.

I had forgotten to be scared for my life.

30

Monday, October 9th, 7 p.m.

If George had called the hit, why was I walking around as if I were off the hook? And even if it wasn't George, the circumstances were still the same: someone wanted me dead and I wasn't.

Needing some of Nelson's off-kilter wisdom on the subject, I'd dragged him to Donny's for a powwow.

Donny looked twenty years older and ten pounds lighter since I last saw him. Good thing Donny had been bald for thirty years, because his lack of hair would have made it more obvious to everybody he was battling cancer. Despite his condition, he still had his sense of humor.

"I got another one for our list of stupidity," he said.

"I got one, too. What's yours?"

"Fireworks."

"Good one," I said. "How about adults who sunbathe?"

"Yes! Even worse, adults who wear Santa hats."

"That's a category killer," I said. "All these people should be like the rest of us and be happy wallowing in their own misery."

"Damn right," Donny said.

"Donny," I started to ask him about his health.

"Whatsup?" He stared right at me, challenging me to bring it up.

"Another Bud?"

"You got it," he said, retreating to the cooler to pull another.

A harsh voice startled me. "Sleeper, how you feeling?"

"Not bad, Simon," I said. The shooting had delayed me from giving Cindy's pimp any updates about George.

"So I hear you took a little lead," he said, sitting down.

"Define 'a little?'"

"Whether or not you're still breathing."

"Point taken," I said, and took a swig of my Bud.

"So how we doing on the Cindy thing? I hear they're looking at the boxer," he said.

"Where did you hear that?"

"I know some people, too."

"You can forget that one. I was with him at Newman's the night of the murder," I said.

"That's quite a coincidence, isn't it?"

"Not particularly." I looked down at my wound.

"That bullet have something to do with this?" Simon asked.

"Could be."

"George?"

"Could be," I said. I'd protected George long enough. I couldn't keep ignoring the evidence, no matter how much my gut disagreed. He had motive, and from what I'd learned about Sniffles, opportunity.

"That dirty old man," Simon said.

"I said it could be George. I'm not sure."

"Who else then?"

140

"I don't know," I said, then, trying it out loud for the first time just to hear how it sounded, "Jim Jones?"

Simon threw his head back and let out a loud chortle. "You're a fucking card, Sleeper." He stood up and slapped a five on the bar. "Thanks for the help."

My sarcasm monitor must have been shot by Sniffles, too, because I couldn't tell if Simon was joking or not.

"Isn't he a drop of rain," Nelson said, after the door shut behind Simon.

"More like a bucket," I said.

"So I saw the punks who rolled me the other day," Nelson continued.

"Where?"

"Down at Hollywood Billiards, casing some guy. Probably robbed him the minute he walked out."

"You tell the cops?" I asked.

"No. We know where my records are. What's the point?"

"The point is they'd go to jail."

"And if they don't? Guess who gets a second beating. Not sure if you've noticed, but the cops don't seem to care much what happens in the T.L. Not all of us can be Dirty Harry like you."

Nelson, as usual, crystallized what I instinctively knew and came to Donny's to hash out. Which crimes the cops pursued in the T.L. was decided, at best, capriciously. I'm a prime example. Not one minute was going to be wasted investigating who shot me. If I wanted to protect myself from Christano and whoever hired him, it would be up to me.

31

Tuesday, October 10th, 8 a.m.

Yuri drove me over to George's office in the Mission first thing the following morning. The sun had already scared off the fog, not uncommon in the fall or in this part of town, making everyone else friendly, almost chipper.

Well, almost everyone.

With no appointment scheduled, I arrived at 8 a.m. to try and catch George before he started his day. To my horror, he was already in a meeting. Did people really live like this? I rested my head against the wall and waited. Through my sleepy haze, I recognized the voice of the man meeting with George. It wasn't hard. Supervisor Harvey Milk now possessed the most recognizable voice in San Francisco. By all accounts he was funny, charismatic, and irrepressible.

Christ, I hated him.

Not because he was any of those qualities, though who really likes an irrepressibly upbeat person? My problem with Milk was the letter supporting Jim Jones he sent to President Carter slandering Grace Stoen. Ever since I read that letter, my dislike of Milk had been festering and I finally

142

understood why. Instead of making the personal political, Milk had made politics personal.

George and the supervisor emerged from his office shaking hands and laughing. George was so enthralled with Milk that his bubbly demeanor remained intact even after he spotted me waiting.

"Sleeper, you know Harvey?" George asked.

"I haven't had the pleasure," I replied.

"Nice to meet you," Milk said, extending his hand.

My hands remained in my pockets. "Sorry, I can't do that."

Milk withdrew his own, puzzled.

"Don't worry, Harvey. Sleeper never learned to play well with others." George said.

"Grace Stoen," I said.

Milk's face went slack.

"Who?" George asked.

"The woman Supervisor Milk slandered in a letter to President Carter. In support of Jim Jones, I should add," I said.

"Nobody knows for sure who the father of that kid is," Milk said.

"Yet you took that psychopath's side over the mother."

"Look, I don't know who you are," Milk's tone sharpened, finding his footing, "but there is no bigger or louder supporter of gay rights in this city than Jim Jones. And he was there for us early. So don't lecture me about what type of person Jim Jones is."

"What the hell does gay rights have to do with Grace Stoen's child?" I asked.

Harvey smiled knowingly, as if he'd finally figured me out. "You know, I used to feel the same way about politics as you do."

"How's that?"

"Condescending."

"What changed?"

"I decided to run for office. Alliances aren't as cut and dried as they appear from your safe vantage point."

I stared at him and shrugged, the argument reaching its natural endpoint.

"If it helps, tell Ms. Stoen I'm sorry," Milk said.

"I'm not telling her a goddamn thing," I replied. "If you want to apologize to her, why don't you write another letter to the President."

Milk ignored me and turned to George. "We'll talk soon, George. Congrats again," he said.

Milk walked away, his first steps slow and careful, but by the time he reached the door his gate had resumed its determined, confident rhythm.

"Sleeper," George said, gesturing me into his office, "you do make things interesting. I'll give you that."

"Mind if I sit?" I asked.

"Sure."

I eased myself into the brown leather chair against the wall.

"What's with the grimace?" George asked.

"Someone put a slug in my lung."

"Why?"

"Poker game argument," I said.

"Caught bluffing?"

"You could say that."

"You here to apologize about the last time we spoke?" he asked.

"Apologize for what?"

"For saying I killed Cindy. For lying about the blood in

144

the apartment."

"Not exactly," I said.

His affable demeanor soured. "No? What then?"

"Well, the cops don't think that my shooting had anything to do with a poker game. In fact, they think you might have had something to do with it."

George clapped and let out a laugh. "Oh, this ought to be good. Go on."

His exuberance flustered me. "Well, the guy who shot me is a guy you know. Charlie Christano."

"Charlie Christ shot you? You bluffed the wrong guy, pal."

"The police think you put him up to it," I said.

"'The first chapter of fools is to hold themselves wise.' And why was I supposed to have done this?"

"Their theory is that you and I conspired in Cindy's murder and now you're tying up loose ends."

"Since you know that's not true, what's your theory?" he asked.

"My theory is that it's awfully coincidental that I was shot by a button man with union ties a few weeks after I accuse you of killing her. The thought that you're involved in this did cross my mind."

George reached into the bottom drawer of his desk, pulled out a bottle of Old Crow, and poured a couple of fingers in two glasses. He pushed one across the desk at me, then leaned back in his chair. "When you say it like that, I have to admit it looks pretty suspicious," he said.

"It does, doesn't it?"

"It doesn't make it any more true, though. So I'm going to tell you man to man: I didn't kill Cindy and I didn't try to kill you." He raised his glass in my direction and shot down the bourbon.

I downed a good glug of mine, the bourbon a touch too sweet for my scotch-trained palate. "You denied all of this before," I said. "But now that I've been shot I was hoping for a little more than your word."

"Like what?"

"Like if you didn't send Christano, who did?" I asked.

"How the hell am I supposed to know? He's a freelance guy. Could be anyone."

"Hmm."

"Sleeper, you have to know the cops asked me about Cindy, in much more detail and under much more duress," George said.

"I don't know anything."

"I'll humor you anyways. If I had killed Cindy, don't you think they would have arrested me by now? Trust me, they want to. But they can't change the fact that after I left Cindy that night, I went to Alfred's with the union brass from Sacramento. The maître de and three waiters all confirmed these facts to the police."

"Why didn't you tell me this before?" I asked.

"Why would I tell you anything?"

"Hmm."

"Besides, I have another reason not to send Christano after you," he said, pouring himself another finger.

"What's that?"

"'Our remedies oft in ourselves do lie, which we ascribe to heaven.'"

"You'll have to translate that one for me," I said.

He took a long sip of his bourbon. "I'm getting out."

"Out of what?" I asked.

146

"This job."

"When?"

"Soon. I'm moving back to Montana with my wife. I'm gonna go fly fishing and play with my grandkids."

"That why Milk was congratulating you?"

George nodded.

"How come you're leaving now?"

"Because I'm a dinosaur. My way of doing things is over; a handshake doesn't mean what it used to. The last thing I'd want to do now is go to jail for ordering the murder of a civilian like you."

"How are you gonna beat the Justice Department?"

"I know how to play the game," he said.

"So do I."

"How's that?"

"If you want to take yourself off the hook, you gotta put someone else on it who's bigger than you," I said.

"You should have been a politician."

"Too many ugly babies in the world. Look, I'm not blowing smoke up your ass, but there aren't many tanks bigger than yours at the aquarium."

"There are a couple," he said.

"Mind giving me a preview?"

He stood up and put on his coat. I followed his lead, struggling to my feet. "Did you vote in the last city election?" he asked.

"Yes," I lied.

"Couple thousand votes the other way and John Barbagelata is our mayor."

"So?" I asked.

"So, that Moscone sure is a lucky guy."

Moscone? What could George have on the mayor?

"You're right about one thing," I said.

"What's that?"

"If you're talking about giving them Moscone, you aren't giving them a fish. You're giving them a whale."

32

I tried to work out what George could have on Moscone. He implied election fraud, but George would have to implicate the union if that was the case. I didn't think George would burn down the thing he'd built in order to go fly-fishing. Could Moscone have been a client of Cindy's? I didn't think so. Everyone knew Moscone played around, but Cindy wasn't Moscone's type. Our mayor was known for preferring women of a darker complexion.

I wanted to be alone at my sanctuary, the racetrack, to mull over the situation. I stopped by Newman's to see if Billy wanted me to place a bet for him.

When I arrived I heard Alfredo taunting someone inside. His tone was sharper than usual, more severe. It wasn't the typical boxing trash talk heard everyday at the gym.

"You want some, too, motherfucker," Alfredo shouted. "Come on, man. Get some."

I turned the corner and saw Sergeant Porto, Stezak's number two, splayed on the ground. Alfredo was dancing over him in street clothes, challenging Stezak to make a

149

move. Stezak pulled his nightstick from his belt. Once Porto regained his footing, the two of them would eventually overpower Alfredo.

"Why don't we at least make it a fair fight," I interrupted. Everyone turned around.

"Your call," Stezak said, his eyes sparkling.

Porto stood up and surprised Alfredo, clutching him from behind. Stezak spun around and struck Alfredo on the hip. "Don't you ever lay your hand on a police officer again," Stezak warned. He took another swing at Alfredo's ribs.

I crossed the room and held back Stezak's arm. Stezak turned and kneed me in the groin. "You either," he ordered.

I doubled over and he cracked me on the back, forcing me to the floor. Having been in this same position with Stezak a year ago, I rolled away to avoid the ensuing blows. I reached under the ring and snatched the pushbroom that Billy stored there. I placed the head on the floor and cracked it off, a sharp, jagged point replacing it.

"Guess who's got the biggest stick now," I said.

"But not as long as mine," Porto said, pulling out his gun while holding Alfredo with his other arm. "Put it down," he ordered.

"Let Alfredo leave," I said. I'd been beaten by Janks, bitten by a psychotic woman, and shot by a mafia hit man. What difference would one more flogging make?

"You're in no position to negotiate," Stezak said.

"Let him go and I'll put it down. Otherwise you'll have to shoot me. This whole situation gets a lot messier if that happens."

I'm thankful I never had to learn Stezak's decision. The door opened and footsteps echoed in the hall.

"Yo, Fredo, you here?" Ricky rounded the bleachers, freezing as he took in the scene. "What's going on?" He pulled off his jacket to enter the fray.

"Alright, settle down everybody," Stezak said. "We're leaving." Porto eased toward the door, keeping his gun pointed at me. Stezak turned to Alfredo. "You do as we ask and everything will be fine."

"Fuck that shit," Alfredo said.

"Don't be foolish. Talk to your brother. Maybe he can talk some sense into you. Whatever you do, don't listen to this fuck-up," Stezak said, pointing to me. "We'll be back before the fight."

The two of them backed out of the gym.

"You okay?" Ricky went to Alfredo and inspected his ribs.

"I'm fine," Alfredo said, pulling down his shirt.

"What did he want?" I asked.

"He told me I had to throw the fight against Virgil. If I don't, he said he'd throw me in jail for murdering that girl."

Stezak's angle had emerged at last: money. I was almost disappointed in his lack of creativity.

"He can't do that. He doesn't have any evidence," I said.

"He has my necklace. Said he found it at the scene."

"He's bluffing," I replied.

"He showed it to me."

"How did he get that?" Ricky asked.

"How am I supposed to know? But it was the gold necklace from my first communion. I thought I left it at this crazy *chica's* house."

A flash of doubt struck me. Had Alfredo's talent blinded me to the possibility that he did it? No, I thought. I saw him the night of the murder at Newman's. There was no better

151

alibi than that.

"Alfredo, maybe we should think about throwing it," Ricky said.

"What?" Alfredo said.

"Yeah, what?" I chimed in.

"What other option do we have? Fredo can't go to jail," Ricky said. "It's only one fight."

"There are options." I said. "Besides, Stezak's a bully. It won't only be one fight."

"What other options?" Ricky asked.

"To start, let's go see this crazy *chica*. See if she gave the necklace to Stezak."

"You cool with that, Fredo?" Ricky asked.

"Yeah. Do it," he replied.

"Alfredo," I said. "We have a week before the fight. I'll figure something out. You didn't do it, you got nothing to worry about."

"Easy for you to say, *muchacho*," Alfredo said.

It *was* easy for me to say. It was harder for me to believe.

33

Tuesday, October 10th, 3:30 p.m.

Mercedes Ledesma lived with her family in a five-story apartment building on 21st and South Van Ness. The stark building was gray and white with small, street facing balconies, most of which were used for either storage or laundry. The younger kids kicked a soccer ball in the ragged courtyard while the teenagers congregated against a wall, shouting at each other in a combination of English and Spanish.

Mercedes' *abuela* answered the door and Ricky handled the introductions in Spanish. We were accompanied down a narrow, bowed hallway to a closed door covered with photos of Erik Estrada. Ricky knocked and the Latina Farah Fawcett answered in jean shorts and an aqua tank top. Even in the warm autumn, the Mission was the one neighborhood in the city where the temperatures allowed for that type of scant clothing.

Though only two years younger than Alfredo, she looked like what she was, a high school kid. It was easy to forget this fact with Alfredo, whose mature body and talent belied his youth. To be fair, Mercedes' figure was capable of bely-

153

ing a few things as well.

"Where's the necklace?" Ricky asked, disregarding any pleasantries.

"What necklace?"

"Alfredo's. He says he left it here." Ricky turned and locked the door.

"I don't know what you're talking about," She lay down on her bed.

"Don't lie to me." Ricky said. I agreed with his assessment of her denial. Teenagers always overrate their acting ability. "Stand up." He grabbed her ankle.

"Hey, don't touch me," she whined.

"Give me the necklace," Ricky said.

"I don't have it. I sold it."

"To who?"

"A girl at school. She gave me twenty dollars. Your brother Alfredo is an asshole."

"What's the name of the girl you sold it to?"

"Maria."

"Maria, huh?" Ricky repeated, then pulled her by the ankles to the end of the bed and grabbed her hair. "Don't lie to me. You gave the necklace to the police, didn't you?"

"The police? What are you talking about?" she shrieked.

"You're lying to us. Where is the fucking necklace?" Ricky dragged her across the room by her hair and smacked her across the face.

"I don't have it," she said, spitting at him. Ricky clenched her neck and pushed her back onto the bed. He balled up his fist as she squirmed underneath him.

"Help," she gurgled.

I grabbed Ricky from behind and pulled him off of her.

"No, Ricky! That's enough."

Ricky was sweating and gasping for air. I thought for a moment he was hyperventilating until he wiped his brow and took a deep breath. Mercedes' grandmother banged on the door, shouting in Spanish.

"Get out!" Mercedes screamed.

Ricky yanked the door open and stormed out.

"We don't want the necklace if you have it," I tried in my most polite tone. "You can keep it. Just tell me, did you give it to the police?"

"Get out!" she shouted back at me, as her grandmother smacked me repeatedly on the shoulder.

Out on the sidewalk, Ricky had cooled down, while my blood was still simmering.

"What the hell was that about?" I yelled.

"What?" Ricky answered. "She was lying to us."

"She's a kid. You can't hit her like that."

"She's fine," he said. "What? You don't think she was lying?"

"She was lying," I agreed. "But you can't do that, Ricky."

"It's my brother who could go to jail. I'll do what I want," he said. "So now what?"

"Now, I get a drink." I was still disgusted with what I'd witnessed. "Alone."

Some people put their thinking caps on; I opt for my thinking drink, a martini. Ricky dropped me off at Donny's, who pours a good one.

The bar was mostly empty, with a smattering of zonked out drunks occupying a few tables.

"Why so serious?" Donny asked.

"Our neighborhood tyrant, Stezak."

"I hate that motherfucker. He's been shaking me down for twenty years. What's he doing now?"

"He's after Alfredo. Trying to get him to lay down in his next fight."

"He has to dirty up everything in the T.L.," Donny said.

"And everybody is scared of him. Afraid of payback."

"I'm not," Donny stated.

"No?"

"Twenty years, man. Enough is enough." I could feel his animosity toward Stezak radiating off of him.

"Let me ask you something, Donny. Would you go on record with the FBI about the shakedowns?"

"Why not?" He coughed again, his lungs sounding like a bagful of pennies.

"You sure? What if nothing comes of it? Stezak might want revenge," I said.

"Look, Sleeper. I don't care. Don't make me spell it out for you why not."

"Okay. Let me talk to a guy. Maybe you and I can take Stezak off the streets for good."

34

Ray Maguire at the FBI sat down across from me in the same drab conference room where we'd met a couple of months ago. He took a sip from a coffee mug that at one time was white, but whose inside was now stained the color of tree sap. Given Maguire's droopy eyes and his stubbled face, I estimated his coffee habit at three pots a day.

"I've got two minutes. You ready to talk to us about what you have on Stezak now?" he asked.

"I already told you, I don't know anything," I said.

"Don't—don't lie to me. So what do you want?"

"I have someone else who is ready to roll on Stezak. Somebody who's not scared of him."

"What's he gonna roll on him about?"

"Shakedowns. Protection money. Twenty years worth."

"How much we talking?" Maguire asked.

"Fifty dollars a month. In that ballpark. He does it to every business in the T.L. My guy says he'll wear a wire, whatever you want."

"That's nice of him." He closed his folder and tapped his

157

pen on the table. "Anything else?"

"What more do you need?" I asked.

"You think we're gonna spend hundreds of man hours investigating Stezak and then settle for fifty dollar shake-downs? And don't talk to me about Al Capone and taxes. That was a whole different situation."

He took my retort right out of my mouth. "He'd go to jail," I said.

"How would you know?"

"I have a friend in the D.A.'s office."

"Then you should take it to him," he said.

"You want headlines or Stezak out of commission?"

"Both," Maguire said.

"Well, it looks to me like you're getting neither."

I took Maguire's advice and treated Hammersmith to a cup of coffee and a cigarette at Sontiya's.

"You're not gonna stop smoking those things, even with one lung?" Hammersmith asked.

"Bullet or cigarette, what's the difference? So, what do you think?"

"Before we get to that, I wanted to give you some good news. You know we're still working with Justice on pros-ecuting George, right?"

"Yeah?"

"Well, I asked them about what Hackett told you, that Cindy turned on George. Not true. He was lying to you."

"I should have known. Thanks for doing that. Now what about Stezak?"

"Why is Donny so willing to put himself out there on this?"

"He won't say it, but he's dying. My guess is lung cancer."

Hammersmith glanced at my cigarette. "Shut up already, Nanna. You think Freitas will go for it?" I referred to Hammersmith's boss, D.A. Joseph Freitas.

"Probably not."

"Probably *not*? Why, not flashy enough for him, either?"

"No. It's big enough for us. The problem is that Stezak knows where all the bodies are buried in this city. He's pretty much off-limits."

"I thought Freitas was clean, relatively speaking," I said.

"He is."

"So?" I asked.

"Moscone wouldn't allow it."

"That's the second time I've heard Moscone's name in an unflattering light in the last twenty-four hours. What's Stezak got on him?"

Hammersmith swallowed more coffee. "Here's how it goes. Back in the early sixties, when Stezak was coming up, he was the night captain for the Northern District, which includes the Western Addition. One night, two vice cops bring in a clean-cut white guy who was with some hooker at the New Yorker Hotel on Fillmore Street. The guy claimed to be a state senator. The vice cops thought he was a lunatic."

"But Stezak knew it was Moscone," I said.

"You got it. Stezak lets Moscone walk, and makes a friend for life."

"So, all it takes to commit crimes with impunity in San Francisco is to let a state senator off on a vice charge?" I asked.

"It is if that state senator goes on to become mayor. I also doubt it's the last time Stezak has cleaned up after Moscone since then," Hammersmith said.

"Freitas needs Moscone's permission to prosecute a corrupt cop?"

"Call it a gentleman's agreement."

"I've got another name for it," I said.

"What's that?"

"I'd call it pimping."

35

Thursday, October 12th, 2 p.m.

Maguire and Hammersmith left me no choice. If they wouldn't protect Alfredo from Stezak, I would. The deal I was about to make couldn't be made at the police station. It would have to wait until Stezak's afternoon cigar stroll.

Stezak's midday walks were well known in North Beach. Everyday after lunch, he and Sergeant Porto moseyed along Broadway Street, perusing the strip clubs, X-rated magazine stores, encounter studios, and dive bars, and more often than not partaking in one or more of the street's offerings.

I followed them into the Hungry I, not the legendary, uncapitalized comedy club, but the skin joint that bought the name after the original closed. It took a full minute for my eyes to adjust to the darkness of the club. On stage, a middle-aged woman ambled around, making no pretense of dancing. The quality of the daytime stripper shows on Broadway was nothing like what you'd find at the Mitchell Brothers at night. If the dancers at the Mitchell Brothers were Major Leaguers, the women at the Hungry I were Double-A at best.

A small orange circle materialized on the opposite side of the club. Stezak's cigar. I squinted and made out his bulging outline leaning against the wall.

I sidled up next to him. "They should start a neighborhood redevelopment project on her stomach," I said.

Stezak looked at me and took another drag of his cigar. "Wait until you're my age. She might as well be Sophia Loren," he said. "Is this a chance encounter?"

"No," I replied.

"I didn't think so. What do you want now?"

"Same thing I always want, for you to lay off Alfredo."

"I'm tired of this conversation. Nice diversion with George, by the way. As you know, it was a dead end."

"I actually didn't know that until recently. But I do know what you told Alfredo yesterday. I'm not gonna let him take the fall for this, in or out of the ring."

"What's so special about him that he can't take one fall?" Stezak asked.

"What's so special is that Alfredo is the rarest thing in the world. He's great."

"How romantic. And how do you plan on stopping me?" he asked.

"By giving you information. The most valuable information anyone has ever given you," I said.

"That's a bold claim."

"Yeah, well I need a promise in advance that if you agree with my assessment you'll let up on Alfredo."

He puffed on his cigar, thinking. "Fine," he agreed, knowing full well he could renege on the deal without consequence.

"And one more thing," I added.

"You're pushing it."

"I want Alfredo's necklace back."

"This better be fucking good," he said.

"It is." I took a deep breath. *Alfredo, I hope you aren't lying to me.* "The FBI has you under surveillance."

"What?"

"They have you under surveillance. Phone taps, tails, the works," I said.

"How do you know?"

"Because they told me."

"The FBI told *you* that I was under their surveillance?"

"Crazy, but yeah," I said.

"Why would they tell you?"

"Because they had you on tape threatening my life and they wanted me to flip on you," I said.

"About what?"

"About that mess last year with Phil Matthews."

"And you didn't flip?" he asked.

"No."

"Why not?"

"Personal reasons," I said.

"What personal life do you have?"

"That's why they call it personal. Now, is it enough to get you off Alfredo's back?"

He took a long puff. "If it's true, yeah," he answered.

"And the necklace?"

He nodded his head.

"When?"

"Go over to Mr. Bing's. If you're story checks out, I'll have Porto drop it off."

"When?"

"Soon. Have a few drinks while you wait, on me."

An hour and three Buds later, Porto walked into Mr. Bing's with an envelope in his hand. He sat down next to me at the bar and, in uniform, ordered a shot of vodka. He handed me the envelope. Judging by its weight, it contained a gold necklace. Porto also pulled out a broken calculator from his pocket and laid it on the bar.

"What's that?" I asked.

"It's where the Feds hid the bug." The bartender placed his shot down in front of him. "So this is about Cindy Teague?"

"Yeah. Stezak told you what happened?" I asked.

"I pieced it together. Too bad. She seemed like a nice girl."

"You knew her?" I asked.

"A little bit. We busted her a couple of times," he said.

"Why bother?" I asked.

He tossed back the rest of his vodka. "Because it's our job." He slapped me on the back as he exited, leaving the calculator parts scattered on the bar.

Newman's locker room was one of the most disgusting places I'd ever set foot in, and I'd placed a shoe in plenty of unsavory spots in my life. Alfredo was in the locker room changing from his boxing gear into his roadwork sweats.

I sat down on the tiny bench next to him and handed him the envelope. He opened it and pulled out his necklace.

"How?"

"It's not important," I said.

"Is it over?"

"It's over."

"He didn't give you the cross?" he asked.

"What cross?"

"The cross that hung on my necklace."

164

"No. No cross." Fucking Stezak. Did I have to specify that I wanted the necklace *and* the charm back? "Don't worry. I'll get that back, too."

"How can I thank you?" Alfredo asked.

"Keep winning."

"That's it?" he asked.

"For the T.L., that's everything."

36

Sunday, October 14th, 11 p.m.

George's ears must have been burning. Two nights later, he showed up at my apartment, dead drunk. It was a rare uneventful night up until that point. I was studying the racing form, my bottle of Johnnie half full, and "Tenderness on the Block" playing on the turntable.

The aggressive pounding on the door startled me enough to retrieve my Louisville Slugger from the closet.

"Open up, Sleeper," George yelled. I could smell the alcohol on him through the door.

"George?" I said, welcoming him in. The only visible indication of his drunkenness was his hat resting on his head half an inch further back than normal.

"You squealed. I hate fucking squealers," he said.

"You're drunk," I replied. "I like drunks."

"Shut up." He said, waved me off.

"Sit down. What's going on, George?" I asked.

"Stezak came to talk to me a couple of weeks ago."

"Yeah?" I asked.

"He said he knew Cindy was talking to the Justice Department. Said he wouldn't say anything if I paid him ten grand. I wonder how he found out about that? You told him, but not me?"

"I did."

He looked surprised by my honesty, hurt.

"But what I didn't know then," I continued, "and what I do now, is that I was wrong. She didn't tell Justice anything. They tried, but she stayed loyal to you."

He sat down in my recliner, inhaled, and closed his eyes. "Are you sure?" he asked.

"Positive."

He exhaled and reopened his eyes. "'The man that hath no music in himself, nor is not mov'd with concord of sweet sounds, is fit for treasons, stratagems, and spoils.' Who are we listening to?" he asked.

"Warren Zevon."

"I used to love music. You know that? Benny Goodman. Glenn Miller."

"I have an Artie Shaw record. Want me to put it on?"

"Would you mind?"

I pulled out "Begin the Beguine," the one song—the one anything—that I had bonded with my father over when I was a boy. George and I listened to the record in its entirety, silent.

"I'm not gonna say I loved Cindy," he started. "There were too many differences. Age—"

"George?" I cut him off.

"Yeah?"

"You don't have to say anything. I don't think you killed her," I said.

"Good. That's all I wanted you to know. Tomorrow I'm

going to talk to the Justice Department and I'll join the ranks of squealers. I hate squealers."

"Can I ask you what you're giving them on Mayor Moscone?"

"You'll have to read the papers like everyone else."

"Not even a hint?"

He struggled to his feet. "All I'll say is that it's a last request from Cindy." He opened the door. "I'm going to pick up the smoking gun right now. Thanks for the Artie Shaw, you fucking rat."

"No problem, you goddamn fink," I said.

He smiled and eased the door shut behind him. I listened for the front gate to bang closed, then returned to studying the form.

Seconds later, two loud blasts, sounding as if they were detonated in my room, shook my windows. I rolled onto the floor and waited. An engine roared and tires squealed. As soon as it was quiet again, I was on my feet and outside.

George lay motionless, face down, on the ground. A handful of Tenderloin gawkers surrounded him, while a pool of blood spread across the sidewalk like syrup over a pancake.

I heard sirens approaching, unsure if they were police or ambulance. If it was the latter, they could slow down and take it easy. Time, for George, was no longer of the essence.

37

Tuesday, October 17th, 11 a.m.

George, having been a San Francisco institution for decades, drew a wide swath of the city into the union hall for his funeral. In the front rows were Mayor Moscone, Willie Brown, and eight of the eleven supervisors, including Harvey Milk. In the back were the members and families from Local 261, as well as representatives from most of the other unions. All the speakers quoted Shakespeare; none of them did it with George's panache.

Buster Lemmer, let out of jail for the occasion, comforted George's wife, Melinda. Funny, I thought, George was such a public person yet I couldn't remember one photo of her in the papers. Of course, in the Triangle, it would have been poor hooker etiquette to mention her by name. She was a young 55, medium height, with an athletic body. She looked like what she was: a cowgirl from Montana who'd lived in San Francisco long enough to acquire the stylings of the big city.

Everyone had a different theory on who killed George and why. The Feds did it, the union did it, the cops did it, it was a robbery gone bad, a mob hit, a suicide-by-murder, a case of mistaken identity. All of them were possible, none probable.

"So what's your theory?" I asked Hammersmith at the reception following the service, also held in the union hall.

"It happened right outside your apartment. Why not you?"

"Don't joke. Stezak might think you're serious," I said.

"My guess would be union infighting."

"Why do you say that?"

"They probably found out he was going to talk to the Feds."

"That's a theory," I said.

"You don't buy it?"

"Nope."

"So what's your take?" he asked.

"You wouldn't believe it if I told you."

"Let's hear it. I need some comedy."

"It's Jones," I said, "and Moscone."

"Congratulations," he laughed, "you are certifiably insane. You think the mayor had Urbancyck killed?"

"I don't know about Moscone, but I'm sure about Jones."

"Why?"

"I think George was going to offer Moscone to the Feds to get them off his back. Right before he died, George implied that whatever he had on Moscone he got from Cindy, which means it has to have something to do with Jones."

"Even if I conceded this as a possibility, which I'm not, do you have any idea of what the connection between Moscone and Jones might be?"

"No," I mumbled.

"Christ, I don't know why I'm telling you this," Hammersmith said, shaking his head. "It will only encourage your rich fantasy life."

"What is it?"

"You don't read the papers much, do you?"

"Just the sports section," I said.

"Right. After the last election, Barbagelata accused the Temple of bussing in people from Redwood City to vote who weren't San Francisco residents. Enough people to sway the election from Barbagelata to Moscone."

"I remember it. I thought they were cleared of those charges."

"They were. But you know who the A.D.A. was who cleared them?" he asked.

"Sports section only, remember?"

"Tim Stoen."

"The guy with the son in Guyana? I met his wife, Grace, at the Concerned Relatives meeting," I said.

"Before he defected, he used to be a muckety muck in the Temple. Jones got Stoen installed in the D.A.'s office, and Freitas appointed Stoen to look into the election fraud. Needless to say, they never found anything. Even worse, the records were destroyed a few months later."

"So how do we prove it?"

"We?" Hammersmith said. "We aren't proving anything. This is your fucked-up windmill. Besides, you have a bigger problem."

"What's that?" I asked.

"If George had killed Cindy, then it made sense for him to sic Christano on you. But if it wasn't George who killed Cindy..."

"Then who sent Christano?"

"And will they sic him again?" Hammersmith added. "Do you own a gun?"

The thought of carrying around a gun made me queasy; getting shot made me dead.

I preferred queasy.

"I can get one."

38

Tuesday, October 17th, 8 p.m.

I went, unarmed, to another wake for George later that night at the Triangle. This one was for George's friends who wouldn't have been welcomed at the formal ceremony. It wasn't particularly sad, nor was it particularly jovial. We left two stools open where George and Cindy normally sat and placed their traditional drinks—Stoli with a twist for George, a Champagne Cocktail for Cindy—on the bar.

An unknown woman entered and the room hushed momentarily. Unknowns were always appraised with suspicious eyes at the Triangle. I should say that she was unknown to everyone in the bar except me, and I only recognized her because I had seen her for the first time earlier that day.

"Is this seat taken?" Melinda Urbancyck asked me.

"It's all yours," I replied.

"White wine," she ordered from Vic, who'd followed her down the bar to her seat. She'd changed from her funeral dress into a casual, black business suit, a white shirt, and a modest string of pearls.

"Am I mistaken that you're Sleeper Hayes?" she asked.

173

"You're not. And you're Melinda Urbancyck."

"I am."

"This isn't the greatest neighborhood to be flashing those pearls, you know. You might want to be careful."

"Please, Mr. Hayes. I've been in much worse dives than this. If you're really concerned, though, I have a driver outside waiting for me." I liked her demeanor, neither crude nor pretentious.

"How do you know who I am?" I asked.

"George was at your apartment before he was shot. It's all in the record. I'm a resourceful gal. So, here I am."

"So you are. And what can I do for you?"

"You were the last person to see George alive. I know you've talked to the police, but I was hoping you could tell me about that night. Why he was there? What he was like?"

"It was nothing important," I said.

"Those were his last moments on earth. They're important to me," she said.

"George came by my apartment to talk. He wasn't happy with me. He thought I'd been disloyal to him."

"Had you been?" she asked.

"Yes."

"Oh." She looked around the bar. "Anything else you can tell me?"

"We listened to an Artie Shaw song."

"George always loved his big band." She composed herself by taking another large sip of wine.

"I have another reason I wanted to meet you," she said.

"Yeah?"

"I wanted to size you up before giving you something."

"And I passed your test this quickly?"

"I've always trusted my instincts." She reached in her purse and laid down a business card on the bar. "I found this in one of George's suit pockets."

I picked up the card and read the name on it. Joe Mazor. The eye-patch wearing spokesman for the Temple.

"Does that name mean anything to you?" she asked.

"It might," I said.

"I thought so. Do what you want with it."

"You sure you don't want to give this card to the cops?" I asked.

"It's one thing to know your husband is being unfaithful. It's quite another for the whole city to know. If the Temple had something to do with his death, I know who pushed him in that direction. There's no reason everyone else should."

"Fair enough," I said.

"Can I ask you one more question?"

"Sure."

"How often was George here?" Before I could give an evasive answer she rescued me. "You don't have to answer that."

I tried anyways. "Look, I didn't know George all that well. I liked him. I think he liked me. That's all I really know about George."

"Thank you for your diplomacy," she said, placing her hand on top of mine.

She reached into her purse, laid a twenty-dollar bill on the bar, and walked out. Vic snapped up the money before it could gather a speck of dust. I wasn't far behind her, my mood suddenly sullen.

Leave it to the widow of a murdered man to kill the buzz at a wake thrown by the friends of his mistress.

39

Thursday, October 19th, 3 p.m.

The problem with someone dying is that it makes you reflect on your foibles, your shortcomings, your regrets—in a word, your life. Who in their right mind likes doing that? I'd gone out of my way to help Alfredo and I wasn't much more than a fan to him. I'd gone way out on a limb for Cindy and I knew her even less. It was time to help someone close. It was time to help Lori.

With Hammersmith's advice to arm myself still clanking around my head, I asked Nelson if I could borrow the .22 he'd bought years ago for protection, but which never left his storage unit in the basement.

"I'm tempted to pull an Andy Griffith on you," he said.

"What's that?" I asked, not being a TV connoisseur like Nelson.

"Andy gave Barney one bullet and made him keep it in his breast pocket, knowing he was a danger to himself and others."

"I see no comparison between Barney Fife and me," I said.

"Neither would Barney."

Even though I didn't like being compared to Andy's inept sidekick, Nelson was probably right. Putting a gun in my hand could not end well.

I left Nelson and went to the Arlington Market for an egg and ham sandwich to go. I hadn't seen Martha since she brought over meals during my convalescence. From behind her counter at the A.M., Martha somehow knew everything that went on in the Tenderloin.

"How you doing, sweetie," I asked, while she fried my egg in a skillet.

"I'm good. You feeling better?"

"Much better. Thanks for helping out while I was sick. Those falafels were a little slice of alright."

"Been a tough few months, hasn't it? Cindy, you, George."

"At least we have Alfredo," I said.

"Hmm," she responded.

"What, no love for Alfredo?"

"Not really."

"Why not?" I asked.

"It's nothing."

"Spill it, Martha."

"What?"

"Spill it," I said.

"Okay, but you didn't hear it from me."

"I never do."

"I heard Alfredo was in a cop car the night of Cindy's murder, right outside her apartment."

"What if I told you I was with Alfredo that night?" I replied. "So it couldn't have been him."

"I'd say the same thing. I heard Alfredo was in a cop car outside Cindy's apartment."

"Far be it from me to argue with you, Martha, but this is one rumor that isn't true."

"I hope not, and anyway—"

"—I didn't hear it from you."

I ate my ham and egg on the steps of the Crescent, then spent the day cleaning up the building, sweeping the hallways, taking out the garbage, and fixing various odds and ends. Anything to kill time before I left to find Lori.

The last time I visited the Chair I was still recovering from being shot and didn't have the strength to stand up to Sal. Now I had the strength, as well as Nelson's piece.

Lori was at the end of the bar, her head slouched to the side, her body hanging off the stool. I sat down next to her and held her hand. The heroin surging through her arteries kept her from recognizing me for ten painful seconds.

"Sleeper?" she said.

"We're leaving," I replied.

Even through her drug-induced haze, I could see the relief in her eyes. She leaned on me and I lifted her off her stool. We were almost outside when Sal noticed what was happening. He cut us off at the threshold.

"Hey, where do you think you're going?" he asked. "It'll cost you twenty bucks."

"I'm not a date," I replied. "But we're leaving."

"The hell you are. I remember you."

"Good," I said, and pulled the gun out of my jacket. "Keep that blade of yours in your pocket and move out of the way." His hand moved toward his knife as he assessed his opponent. "Don't do it." I cocked the gun. "I'll claim self-defense and not one cop in the T.L. is gonna argue with me."

He looked around the room, realizing that none of the

other patrons would rise to his defense, either. "Don't do this," he said. "I'll find you."

"I'll worry about that later."

He held the door open, smiling. "I'll see both of you, soon."

I carried Lori back to her apartment and inspected her works. I flushed the bag of junk on her nightstand down the toilet. She saw what I was doing and screamed, clawing at me.

"I hate you. I fucking hate you," she yelled.

"Do you want to die?"

She collapsed on the bed, wailing at first, then whimpering, before finally passing out from exhaustion thirty minutes later.

I sat on a chair next to her bed, thumbing through her copy of *Zen and the Art of Motorcycle Maintenance*, with one sentence in particular catching my attention. "The truth knocks on your door and you say, 'Go away, I'm looking for the truth,' and so it goes away."

Lori awoke around midnight. "Yes," she said.

"Yes, what?"

"Yes, I want to die," she answered, and fell back asleep.

We both woke up around eight the next morning. She looked at her night table confused.

"I threw it out," I said.

She took a deep breath. "Good."

"Do you want to get clean?" I asked.

"Yes," she said.

"I'm gonna try to make that happen. Promise me you won't answer the door for anyone. Especially Sal."

She nodded her head.

"Promise me," I repeated.

"I promise."

"I'll be back soon," I said.

I craved a drink before meeting with the one person who could help Lori right away, but I resisted. I needed all my faculties for this meeting or I'd be forced to use Nelson's gun after all.

40

Thursday, October 19th, 5:30 p.m.

Wethersby was in a meeting with a client. I told the new but equally ravishing receptionist that I would wait. Tenora spotted me from her cubicle and came out to greet me.

"Hey," she said.

"Hey back." I hardly recognized her in her conservative, professional attire.

"What's going on?" she asked. "You need some legal advice?"

I realized she thought I was here to see her.

"No. I'm here to see Bill Wethersby."

"You know Bill Wethersby?"

"Surprised?"

"I guess I shouldn't be," she said.

"What do you mean?"

"I knew you had something to do with me getting this job."

"I don't know what you're talking about."

Before she could ask her follow-up question, the receptionist rescued me.

"Mr. Wethersby will see you now."

"See you around," I said to Tenora.

"You always do."

I let myself into Wethersby's office and stationed myself opposite him at his broad, polished desk. No comfy couch and drinks this time. I felt like I'd been called into the principal's office for pulling Lisa Chamberlain's ponytail.

"Hello," he said. "What's going on?"

"Nothing much. How's the case against Janko?"

"Oh, that's been dispensed with. The police committed many procedural errors in their search."

Procedural errors. Nice euphemism for a backroom deal.

"Good, I guess." I didn't have time to run around the tree with him. "I was hoping now you could do me a favor."

"That wasn't a favor you did for me. You were compensated," he said.

"Well, I'm asking for one anyway. I have a friend who's in need of rehab."

"Okay."

"She doesn't have any money."

"Okay."

"And she needs help, now."

"Has she tried the Hospitality House on Turk?" he asked.

Was he being obtuse or a prick?

"Hey Bill, enough with the polite bullshit. She needs to get out of the Tenderloin now, and if she doesn't get out and get help, she'll die. I need to know if you have any openings at your facility in Sonoma."

"Does she want the help or do you? Because if she doesn't want it, it won't work. Trust me."

"She wants it," I said.

Apparently those were the magic words.

"Wait here." He walked out of his office and whispered into his secretary's ear.

"She's making a call for you," he said, returning to his desk.

"How's Tenora doing?"

"She's great. Smart. Never complains."

"I told you so," I said.

"Those are your four favorite words, aren't they?"

"They're definitely top ten," I said.

"She's also made a special friend."

"Who's that?"

"She'll have to tell you about that one herself," he said. His secretary came back in and handed him a piece of paper.

"Here," he said to me. "Take this number. Ask for Regina. She'll take care of your friend."

"How much we talking?"

"It's free," he said.

"No strings attached?"

"Stringless. You know my soft spot."

"Shit, man. I wasn't expecting free. Thanks, Bill."

"I hope it works out for your friend."

"Me, too," I said. "So who is Tenora dating?"

"Why, are you jealous?" he asked.

"Hey, I had my chance there," I said.

"All I'll say then is she's set her sights a little higher."

41

Thursday, October 19ᵗʰ, 8 p.m.

I marched right back to Lori's. The clock was ticking. I didn't want her to lose her resolve before she started jonesing again. Even more pressing was Sal, who would be hunting her down soon if he wasn't already.

I packed a suitcase and called Vic. An hour later, before Lori fully understood what was happening, she was on her way to Sonoma.

Even though I'm in full agreement with the wisdom that no good deed goes unpunished, I was surprised at how fast my penalty was meted out.

Janks was pacing in front of the Crescent when I returned. I was pissed off and ready if he wanted another piece of me.

"You ready to fight like a man this time?" I asked.

"We gotta go," Janks said.

"What?"

"We gotta go. Go inside and pack a bag," he said.

A little déjà vu washed over me. Hadn't I just uttered those words to Lori? "I'm not going anywhere with you," I said.

"I know who shot you,"

"I know who shot me, too."

"Yeah, but I know who sent him and he's not going to stop until you're dead," Janks countered.

"Keep talking."

"It was Jones."

"Jim Jones?"

"Yes," Janks answered. "Sleeper, listen to me for one minute. You know I was supplying the Temple with guns. I had to tell them that I got arrested and I gave them your name without thinking. I forgot about it until I heard you were shot. When I asked them if they did it, they didn't say yes, but they didn't say no, either."

"You talk to Jim Jones?"

"Not him, but his person here in the city."

"A woman?" I asked.

"How did you know?"

"Do you meet with her face-to-face?" I asked, ignoring his question.

"No. Telephone."

That at least explained how they found out where I lived.

"I thought Jim Jones handled his security in house."

"You should read the paper. He brags about his mob connections all the time. *The Chronicle* reported he even has a hit list."

"When did you start caring about my welfare? Last time we saw each other, you were trying to kill me yourself," I said.

"I don't like you and you don't like me. But Wethersby told me that you didn't rat me out, so I don't want you dead on account of my mistake. Now, will you go get a bag or not?"

"Where are we going?"

"My warehouse."

"Your warehouse?"

"You got someplace better?" he asked.

The sad fact was, I didn't.

I crammed a couple of sweaters, a pair of cords, jeans, a toothbrush, and Nelson's .22 into a duffel bag.

I stopped by Nelson's room on the way out to let him know I'd be gone for a while.

"You alright?" he asked.

"Yeah," I said.

Nelson and I were friends because we knew that was the only meaningful exchange any two men should ever have with one another.

Janks was still pacing outside waiting for me. "We have to get some food for you. There aren't a lot of options South of Market."

"Food for me? What about you?"

"I'm crashing down in Portrero with a girl."

I reached for his arm. "Janks, this isn't a set-up, is it? You're not calling the cops or dropping me on the pond like a sitting duck for Christano, are you?"

"I swear to you I'm not. I don't know what else to say."

I tried to assess all the possible angles before remembering whom I was dealing with. Stumps don't have many sharp edges.

"Let's go," I said.

After Martha packed up a care package, Janks dropped me off and handed me the key to his warehouse. "I'm sorry I got you into this mess," he said. "We'll figure something out, okay?"

"Okay," I said, but I knew I'd be the one doing all the figuring.

42

Wednesday, October 25ᵗʰ, 1 p.m.

I'd say I spent the next week at Janks's place in the SOMA neighborhood watching paint dry, but since the area was mostly warehouses and parking lots, it was more like watching concrete erode. There was a heavy Asian population in SOMA nearer to downtown and a few hotels housing longshoremen, sailors, and merchant marines, but apart from that, the only real action were the gay clubs on Folsom Street.

I read *Journey into Fear* by Eric Ambler, listened to the transistor radio for music. KYA was still looping ABBA, the Bee Gees, and the *Grease* soundtrack. KSAN was playing a lot of Blondie and the Clash, while KDIA was spinning Earth, Wind & Fire, Rufus, and Roberta Flack.

Yuri picked me up daily in his cab and drove me into the Tenderloin to discreetly perform general upkeep on the Crescent and, due to the lack of running water at the warehouse, on myself. I also checked in on Alfredo, who looked like a new man, training with enthusiasm. Ricky continued to prepare for Ward's heavy right hand by using weights to strengthen Alfredo's neck.

One place I knew Christano wouldn't be was the library. Though it sounded like a lot of bluster to me, *The Chronicle* had run a piece on Jones's alleged mob connections. I couldn't wrap my scotch-soaked brain around the fact that Jim Jones was terrorizing the city all the way from the jungles of Guyana. The article even quoted my interrogator at the FBI, Ray Maguire.

Given the library's proximity to the Federal Building, I popped in to see my pal at the Bureau.

"Mr. Hayes," Maguire said.

"I didn't realize you were in charge of the Jim Jones and Stezak investigations," I said.

"We can juggle more than one ball at a time."

"I came to give you some information about the Jim Jones ball," I said.

"Interesting. I was assuming this was about Stezak."

"Nothing new there."

"You sure about that?" he asked.

"Pretty sure," I replied, confused by his suspicious tone.

"Okay, go ahead. Jim Jones."

"I was shot by a mob guy, Charlie Christano, a few months back. Your pals at Justice tried to convince me that George Urbancyck had hired him. I thought it was garbage at the time, and I'm sure about it now. It was Jones who sent him."

"You know Jim Jones sent him, how?"

Shit. I couldn't tell him how I knew. Twenty-four hours ago I would have flipped on Janks in a heartbeat. Funny how loyalties can change when you're least expecting it.

"I can't tell you that," I said.

"Then I'll add it to the file." He stood up to leave.

"You'll add it to the file? That's it?"

"What else do you want me to do?" he asked.

"I want you to arrest him before he tries to kill me again," I said.

"Let me ask you a question," Maguire said.

"Okay."

"Did you tell Stezak we were monitoring him?"

"Why would I do that?" I asked, my heart paddling.

"I don't know why you'd do something so stupid. But one of our guys saw you go into the The Hungry I with him."

"So we both like naked women, no crime in that."

"After he left The Hungry I, he went back to his office. Soon after that, our bug went dead. Quite a coincidence, don't you think?"

"That's life, isn't it, one big coincidence," I said.

"Cut the crap, Sleeper. I'm not stupid. We know you said something to him. So you'll have to forgive me if we aren't going to go out of our way to help you with your little problem here. Like I said, I'll add it to the file."

"Don't you at least want to know why Jim Jones wants me dead?"

"Fine," he said. "Humor me."

"I think Jim Jones had George Urbancyck and a hooker named Cindy Teague murdered because they knew about something illegal he'd done."

"Like what?" he asked.

"I'm not sure, maybe something about the mayoral election."

"You have any proof for this theory of yours?"

"Not yet."

"And you can't tell me who told you that Jones hired

Christano to shoot you?"

"No," I said.

"Look, I want Jones. You bring me anything on murder or election fraud, we'll take it seriously. Until you have something, though, I can't help."

"So I'm on my own?" I asked.

"That's the way you like it, isn't it?"

"In everything but sex."

"Then you should be okay."

"You sure? It kind of feels like someone's slipping me a Mickey Finn."

43

Wednesday, October 25ᵗʰ, 6 p.m.

For the first time since beginning her rehab, Lori was allowed calls from the outside world. I saw no irony in steeling myself for this phone conversation with a double shot of Johnnie.

"How are you doing?" I asked.

"I'm doing well. Really well."

"Yeah?"

"You know, one day at a time and all that, but good. This is a great place, Sleeper. I don't know how you managed it, but thank you so much for getting me in here."

"No need to thank me. It's what anyone would have done," I said.

"I love that you think that's true. How are you?" she asked.

"Keeping busy. Still trying to figure out this Cindy thing."

"Sleeper, listen. I need to tell you something."

"Okay." Here it was. The predictable and understandable break-up.

"I was in group therapy and something came back to me about the night Cindy died."

"What's that?" I asked, perking up.

"A guy came in the bar and asked for Cindy that night. I couldn't place him at the time, but he looked familiar. I finally realized why. He wasn't in his cop uniform."

"A cop? You sure?"

"Positive."

"You remember what the guy looked like?" I asked.

"Fat guy. Salt and pepper hair. Mustache. He's always around the Tenderloin. I don't know his name."

"That's okay. I do." *Sergeant Porto.*

"You think it means anything? I hope it didn't have anything to do with her dying."

Absolutely, I thought.

"No, I don't," I said. Now that Lori was feeling better, I didn't want any guilt to drive her back into depression, or worse, relapse.

"Really?"

"Really." I could sense her relief over the phone. "Hey Lori?"

"Yeah?"

"I'm glad you called and that you're doing well. I needed some good news."

Lori was quiet, no doubt confused over what passed as openness from me. "You take it easy, okay?" she said.

"Sure," I said. "Easy as Pie."

I slammed Janks's phone down. That snake Stezak. I should have never trusted him. First, he withholds Alfredo's cross, and now this news about Porto.

I'd played enough minor league ball. It was time for me to swing the bat in the big leagues.

44

Thursday, October 26ᵗʰ, 3 p.m.

Enough screwing around. If Stezak didn't tell me everything he knew about the night Cindy was murdered, it wasn't going to be because of any timidity on my part.

I called him from a payphone down the block from Central Station.

"I know who murdered Cindy Teague," I said.

"What are you talking about?"

"I'm at the Keystone. Meet me there and I'll tell you. And come by yourself. No Porto."

He hung up without a reply.

The Keystone Korner, the best jazz club in the city, was situated on Vallejo and Powell, across the street from the station. I ordered a Johnnie and took a corner booth.

Stezak walked in thirty minutes later. The bartender stood at attention as Stezak ambled by and sat across from me.

"Can I buy you a drink?" I asked.

"This isn't a social visit."

"I thought we were pals. After all, I did tell you about the FBI investigating you."

"I don't have pals." He plucked a cigar from his shirt pocket and unwrapped it.

"Fine," I said, "Where's the cross?"

"What cross?"

"The charm from Alfredo's necklace. That cross."

"I don't know what you're talking about."

"You know exactly what the hell I'm talking about."

Stezak chewed his cigar, eyes drilling deep into me. "You can't have called me over here to ask about a necklace I already returned to you. What do you really want?"

"We had a deal about Cindy's murder. You held out on me."

"No. We had a deal about Alfredo, not Cindy's murder. I've kept my end. Ask Alfredo if he's seen any trace of me."

"Porto was looking for Cindy the night she was murdered," I said.

He spit out shreds of moist tobacco onto the table. "I think I'll take that drink now," he said, gesturing to the bartender who brought over a vodka on the rocks. "Keep talking," he said.

"Porto went to the Triangle looking for Cindy the night she was murdered. In civilian clothes," I said.

"What he does on his personal time is none of my business."

"Did Porto kill Cindy?"

"No," he answered, shooting his drink down in one swallow.

"But you know who did, don't you?" I asked.

"Sleeper, I'm giving you a warning. Stop this shit now. You're edging into dangerous ground."

"Who killed her?" I asked.

"Last warning."

"I'm tired of being given warnings. How about I give you

one instead? I already proved to you that I have friends at the FBI. Well, they were plenty pissed at me when they found out I tipped you off about their investigation. I'd really like to get back in their good graces. Maybe if I tell them about Porto murdering Cindy they'll pick him up. Maybe if they pick him up and hang a murder charge on him, your loyal bagman might not be so loyal anymore. Maybe Porto rolls on you to save his ass."

"You shouldn't make any threats you aren't willing to back up," He gnawed his cigar.

"You're leaving me no choice," I said.

"And you, me. Last time, are you going to drop this?"

"Last time. Who killed Cindy?"

Stezak leaned across the table. "You play poker, right?" he whispered.

I nodded my head.

"You know why I don't?" he asked.

"No idea."

"Because I don't bluff." He stood up and picked up his glass. "Remember, you brought this on yourself."

He walked past the bar, handed his glass to the bartender, and stopped in the doorway to light his cigar. Smoke obscured his face as he turned and took one last look at me. He flicked the match on the ground, gratuitously extinguishing it with a turn of his foot.

I had wanted to play in the big leagues. Well, here I was. I proved I could hit a fastball. Now the question was, could I hit a curve?

45

Friday, October 27th, 6 p.m.

Having failed to extract anything of value from Stezak, I refocused on the other sociopath in my life, Jim Jones. If anyone knew whether Cindy had any incriminating evidence on the Temple, it would be one of her fellow refugees at the Human Freedom Center.

I set off for Berkeley to find out. Turning the corner onto Market Street, I was yanked into a doorway, a knife pressed on top my carotid artery.

"Where is she?" Sal asked.

"Where's who?"

"Don't play stupid. Where's Lori?"

"How would I know?"

"I said don't play stupid."

He took the knife from the outside of my neck and placed it on my leg, the tip piercing my jeans and scratching my skin. Pedestrians walked right past us, heads down. Nothing to see here but another Tenderloin mugging.

"I only saw her one night. After that I don't know."

He pushed the knife three inches into my leg. I let out

a scream that he muffled with his other hand. If you ever have the choice of being shot or stabbed—two sensations I'd recently had the displeasure of experiencing—take the bullet every time. While I have vague memories of being shot in the chest and losing half a lung, I don't think I'll ever forget the feeling of a knife slicing through the tendons and muscles of my quadriceps.

"Take what I got in my pocket for that night. She was no good anyway," I said.

"Fuck off. I ain't stupid. If you want her out of the life, it's gonna cost you more than twenty bucks." He reached in my pocket and took out eleven dollars. "I'll take this as a down payment. You owe me a thousand more."

"Come on, man. I don't know where she is."

He twisted the knife around in my leg, the scraping of steel on bone triggering an eruption of vomit.

"Good. Because I like cutting people up almost as much as I like money," he cackled, and bopped down Larkin Street, whistling.

I was treated at the St. Francis emergency room by the same doctor who had operated on my gunshot wound. This time, though, Dr. Gallo sent me back to Janks's warehouse the same day, with a vial of painkillers. Those pills, and a bottle of whiskey, helped me through the worst of the short convalescence.

Two days later I limped to my initial destination, the Human Freedom Center.

Jeannie opened the door, noted the bottlecap-sized spot of blood on my jeans that had spread during the BART ride over. "What happened?"

I sensed her fear that my state of disrepair was related to my last visit here. "Nothing to do with you folks," I said.

"Good." She looked both directions before closing the door. "Please, come in."

"You okay?" I asked. "You seem a little tense."

"We had a break-in last night. No doubt the Temple. They stole all the files they could get their hands on."

"Anything important?"

"No. We know their tactics better than anyone. We don't store anything valuable here."

"Can we talk alone?"

"Can it wait until our support meeting is over? We're wrapping up," she said.

"Would you mind if I sat in again? The more people I throw this at, the better."

"Come on in," she said.

The group greeted me like a long lost son. Everyone from the last meeting was there, plus a couple of new faces.

"Most of you know Mr. Hayes," Jeannie began. "For those of you who don't, he was a friend of Cindy's who is looking into her murder. As you all know, it's still unsolved." This caused everyone's eyes to either glisten, stare at the floor, or both. "Please, Mr. Hayes, go ahead."

"I'll get right to it. I don't have anything concrete on her murder, but everywhere I turn, it comes back to Jones." I knew this wasn't what they wanted to hear. "My theory so far is that Cindy was willing to go public with something, either to the Justice Department or to the press, or both."

"Oh, Lord," Wanda gasped. "Any idea what it was about?"

"I think it might have something to do with the mayoral election."

"How so?" Grace asked.

"I'm thinking voter fraud. The problem is proving it. All the records were destroyed." I halted, remembering that Grace's ex-husband had led the D.A.'s investigation exonerating the Temple of any wrongdoing.

"You don't have to dance around the issue," Grace said. "Tim was the A.D.A. on the case."

"You think Cindy might have had some kind of proof about the election?" Jeannie said.

"I think so. Did Cindy ever say anything to the rest of you about going public?"

Everyone shook their heads, except one of the new faces, Debbie, who looked off to the side.

"No offense, Mr. Hayes," Al said, "but do you think Jim Jones would kill over voter fraud?"

"You guys know better than me. All I know is the last friends Jones has in San Francisco are the politicians. If he ever wants to return, he can't afford to lose them. What do you all think?"

"I think Jim Jones would kill anyone he thought betrayed him, no matter how large or small the reason," Jeannie said.

"All I'm trying to find out is what happened to Cindy," I said. "I think I'm close. If any of you know something, you can tell me."

I looked at Debbie, who, like Grace and Jeannie, would turn even the stiffest neck. What was it with all these Temple broads? If part of Jim Jones's plan was to recruit hot, young co-eds, mission accomplished.

"I think I know what it was," Debbie whispered.

"It's okay," Jeannie said. "You can talk to Sleeper. What did Cindy tell you?"

199

"It's something I told her. Do you know who Michael Prokes is?" she asked me.

"No," I said.

"Michael Prokes is the Temple's P.R. guy," Debbie said, "and Jones's closest confidante."

"Okay," I said.

"Before joining the Temple, Michael was a journalist." I noticed her use of his first name. She and Prokes were intimate. "He's a true believer, but he's also a journalist. He keeps meticulous notes for posterity. Maybe for a book, I don't know. When I left, I grabbed two of his notebooks and stuffed them into my bag. Then I...I gave them to Cindy." She closed her eyes in a failed attempt to block her tears.

"What did they have in them?" I asked.

"A bunch of praise for Jones mostly. But there were also details of Jones's meeting with Moscone."

"What meeting?"

"The meeting where Moscone asked for Jones's support in the election," she said.

"And?"

"And Jones is very upfront about his demands. He wanted a high-profile appointment and more representation on government boards for Temple members. In return, Jones guaranteed a Temple turnout for Moscone."

"A legal one?"

"By any means necessary."

"The mayor knew the score?"

"According to Prokes."

"Did Cindy tell you where she hid the notebooks?" I asked.

"No, and I don't want to know."

"She probably kept it at our private investigator's office,"

Jeannie offered. "It's where we keep anything valuable."

"The guy with the eye patch?"

"Yes. Joe Mazor."

"How about Prokes, any chance I can meet with him?" I asked.

"Sure," Debbie said. "You going to Guyana anytime soon?"

46

Monday, October 30th, 12 p.m.

Debbie's information might be more helpful than she knew. George had been carrying around one of Mazor's cards. If Mazor was holding Cindy's file on Prokes, it had to have been Mazor who George was meeting with the night he died to obtain, as George had called it, "the smoking gun."

Janks's lack of a bathroom had become onerous. Tired of pissing in a bucket, I finished my business and walked outside in my boxers to dump the contents. I opened the door and slung the urine. Just my luck, it landed on a cop dressed in full riot gear.

"Get down on your knees!" one of the other, non-piss stained cops shouted from behind his mask. "Get down on the ground. Now!"

I assumed the position. They surrounded me, shoving my face in the dirt. I turned my head and twelve hours worth of urine trickled toward me. They cuffed me and kicked me in my ribs, but at least pulled me off the ground before I was forced to get reacquainted with my own bodily fluid.

They drove me a couple of blocks to the Hall of Justice

on 6th and Bryant and ushered me into a barren interrogation room. A few hours later, two plain-clothes detectives joined me.

"I'm Detective Harris. This is Detective Phippen. Do you know why you're here?"

"No," I said.

"We've been monitoring that warehouse for gun running. We want to know what you were doing there."

"I needed a place to crash."

"Are you friends with Curtis Janko?" the fat detective asked.

"No."

"Are you part of his gun running operation?"

"No."

"Convince me."

"No."

"Is that all you have to say?"

"I want my lawyer."

"Fine. We'll call the public defender," he said.

"No thanks. I'll call my own."

"Who's your lawyer?" the short one asked.

"Bill Wethersby."

"Funny guy."

"Give me the damn phone and we'll see who the joker is," I said.

Detective Harris and I sat in silence until Wethersby arrived half an hour later.

"Did you say anything?" Wethersby asked me.

"No."

"Okay," he turned to the detectives. "Are you charging him with anything?" The detectives looked at one another.

"Were there any guns in the warehouse?" Wethersby asked.

"An unlicensed twenty-two."

"It's my pal's," I said.

"Don't talk," Wethersby instructed me. "Anything else?"

"He was smoking a joint when we busted him," shorty said.

"Let's go, Sleeper."

"Where do you think you're going?" fat boy said.

"We're leaving. If you want to charge him with having a joint and his buddy's Saturday night special, go ahead." Neither of them moved a muscle. "That's what I thought."

We stood up, collected my belongings, including Nelson's gun, and walked silently through the labyrinth of corridors to his car. "What happened?" Wethersby asked, after the closing the door to his Jag.

"I needed a place to stay. The guy who shot me is still trying to shoot me."

"Why there?"

"Because Janko is the one who found out who's after me," I said.

"How'd he find that out?"

"Because after you had him raided, he told someone it was my fault. That person put a bounty on my head."

"Who was that?" Wethersby asked.

"Jim Jones."

"Jesus," Wethersby sighed.

"To some," I said.

"Why Janko's? You knew they were monitoring him."

"I didn't have a lot of options after I rented out my ski chalet in Aspen."

"Okay," Wethersby said. "I get it."

"Do you? Because you seem to have forgotten the part

where a guy is trying to kill me because you raided a ware-house in order to protect yourself."

"Alright, alright. You've made your point. I'll make it up to you."

"How?"

"I have a place for you to stay."

We drove north through the Tenderloin and hung a left on California. We U-turned at Hyde, stopping in front of a nondescript, four-story apartment building.

"Come on." Wethersby exited his double-parked car.

We walked up two flights of stairs and into a fully fur-nished one-bedroom apartment straight out of *Better Homes and Gardens*. The living room included a dining area, which opened onto a modern kitchen. I could see my reflection in the hardwood floors dotted with tasteful area rugs. Two stiff looking lounge chairs flanked an uncomfortable looking couch, and the lights of the South Bay blanketed the hills and valleys through the tall, oversized windows.

Wethersby took a key off his key ring and placed it on the counter separating the kitchen from the living room.

"What's this place?" I asked.

"You could call it a timeshare. For emergencies."

"My kind of emergencies."

"Make yourself at home. You won't run into many ten-ants. Most of these units are timeshares. If you do, keep your head down. Anyone else living here is like you."

"Witness Protection?"

"Exactly."

"I'm not big on small talk, anyway."

"Bell Market will deliver food. Put it on my tab, but don't abuse it. If you absolutely need to leave, the Hyde Out is a bar that I imagine is right up your alley. But try your best to stay put and not do anything stupid until I think of some way out of this."

I surveyed my new surroundings. "Take your time."

47

Thursday, November 2nd, 9 a.m.

Two days later, after an eyeful of Soap Operas, *Phil Donahue*, and *Scooby-Doo*, I arose from the couch and did precisely what Wethersby warned me against, doing something stupid. I picked up the phone and asked Janks to locate Christano. I needed to be prepared in case Wethersby couldn't figure out an escape plan for me. Janks, still feeling guilty about the arrest, agreed.

The following morning, while smoking a nail on the steps of the apartment, a familiar face left the building.

"Hey," I said. "You come to see me?"

Tenora spun around, mortified. She glanced back at the door. "What are you doing here?" she asked. "Why are you always around?"

"I'll take that as a 'no.' How's the job?"

"It's good. Listen, I can't talk now. I'll see you." She walked to the curb and hailed a cab.

"Wait!" I yelled. "Let's talk now."

"No, really, I have to go. I'm late for a meeting." She jumped in a taxi and was on her way downtown before I could proposition her properly.

What the hell was that? I leaned against the steps and took another pull from my cigarette. A few drags later, my question was answered. A black town car pulled up and Mayor Moscone, fumbling with his tie, exited the building and glided into the backseat.

The lurid calculus was simple enough. Moscone was known for having a string of black girlfriends dating back decades. Moscone was a client of Wethersby's. Wethersby had told me that Tenora had made a "special friend" at work. All of that totaled a morning tryst at a love nest on California Street.

Tenora was a fast learner. A couple of years ago she'd swapped her black liberation theology for the hippie life-style. Now it appeared she had jettisoned both to become ensconced in the city's political establishment.

Either that or she'd genuinely fallen for our charming mayor.

Whatever the reason, Tenora was on the fast track to success and, I feared, heartbreak.

48

Friday, November 3rd, 2 p.m.

Moscone and Jones. Jones and Moscone. Was I focusing on the wrong guy? Could it have been Moscone who wanted to keep the election fraud quiet? As jaded as I was, I didn't think our mayor would stoop to murdering his critics. That still seemed like the purview of Jim Jones.

Joe Mazor was the one I was counting on to provide some answers. I'd thumbed through Cindy's file on him before the Temple maniac had burglarized them from my apartment. I remembered wondering at the time why the Concerned Relatives had hired him. Given his background, which included doing time in prison for check kiting, it seemed pretty obvious to me he was a self-promoting media whore.

I called his office to set up an appointment, then phoned Jeannie to enlist her in my plan.

Mazor's office was on the 10th floor of the Russ Building on Montgomery Street. His secretary, a stern looking 60-year-old woman with a bad dye job, was behind a small desk in the outer room. I'd lay 2-1 she was a relative, 3-1 it was his mother.

"Is your son in?" I asked.

"Nephew. Is he expecting you?" she asked.

Mazor heard the conversation through the open door connecting the two rooms and called me into his office. "Joe Mazor. What can I do for you?" he said in his gravelly voice, pumping my hand. His eye patch, absurd looking in photos, was off-putting in person.

"I am a friend of the Concerned Relatives," I said, sitting down across his desk. "I'm sure you heard about the break-in over there?"

"I did," he said.

"Jeannie wanted to double check and make sure all the files about Jones were still intact and safe," I said.

"They are."

"She wanted me to see them with my own eyes," I said.

"I can't do that. Lawyer-client confidentiality."

"You aren't a lawyer," I said. "Call her."

My directness caught him by surprise. After a brief phone conversation with Jeannie he turned around and opened the door to a horizontal filing cabinet, revealing a charcoal-colored safe. He twisted the knob one way, then the next. As he began the final turn, a loud voice from the reception area jolted us both upright.

"I want to see Mazor!" a deranged sounding man shouted.

"He's in a meeting," his aunt replied, and I could see her outline standing up through the frosted window.

"He owes me five thousand dollars. Get him out here!" The man knocked on Mazor's inner door.

Mazor looked confused and embarrassed. He pulled out a pistol from his top drawer and slipped it inside his suitcoat.

"One moment," he excused himself, closing the door into

the waiting room behind him. I rushed around the desk and turned the dial back to the right, waiting for the final click. The shouting from the other room grew louder. At last, the last tumbler fell into place and I opened the safe. It was packed topped to bottom with manila file folders.

The noise in the outer room quieted down. I saw Mazor walk the stranger out, then turn back toward this office. I snatched the top two files and stuffed them into the back of my pants, sitting down before I had a chance to close the safe door.

He returned to his desk and knelt back in front of the safe, the open door momentarily halting him. He looked back at me, then continued. "These are the files. As you can see, they're safe and sound."

"Mind if I take a look at one?" I asked.

"Jeannie didn't okay that."

"Alright," I said, even though I knew she had. "I understand. Jeannie will be relieved. Thanks."

"Whatever you need," he said. "Don't hesitate to ask."

After a few minutes of forced chitchat, we shook hands and I exited the building. I turned right onto Bush and helped Nelson, who'd given the performance of his lifetime in Mazor's office, up the hill.

I returned to Wethersby's apartment, flopped down on the couch, and pulled out the files I'd taken from Mazor. The front of the first read, "Tim Carter." I opened it up and found ten or so sheets of paper in the file.

Everything seemed to be in order, with one exception: none of the papers had any writing on them.

49

Friday, November 3rd, 9 p.m.

Yuri drove me back to the Crescent later that night to check on its condition. Luckily for me, Tenderloin flophouses don't need much managing. Neither did the tenants. Nelson's mood had continued to improve and Lady Ellinger was her regular, ornery self. I missed the place like an amputee misses a lost limb.

I fell back into the front seat of Yuri's cab and rubbed my emotionally drained eyes. "Okay, let's go," I said to Yuri, who stared straight ahead, as motionless as the car. "Turn the key, already. What are you waiting for?"

"He's waiting for his fare to tell him his destination," Stezak said from the backseat. I reclined my head and exhaled, comforted by the fact that unlike most people, I at least knew when my ticket would be punched.

"So, tell him," I said to Stezak.

"Golden Gate Park."

And now I knew the where, as well.

Yuri inched into Hyde Street, then turned west on Sutter. "How bad is this hand?" Yuri asked me.

"Rags."

"For me, too?" he asked.

"Rags all around," I said.

We drove down Gough and turned right on Oak.

"I haven't gone to the FBI," I said to Stezak, in an attempt to change his mind I knew full well was futile. "They can't pin anything on you."

"You're right about that," Stezak said.

"So what's the point of this?"

"I take every threat against me seriously."

"Perfect," I said. "The one time anyone takes me seriously it's you."

"How about those Niners?" Yuri asked.

I would have laughed at Yuri's clueless stab at taxi driver small talk if I wasn't still trying to come up with a plan to save both our necks.

"There has to be some deal we can cut," I said, ignoring Yuri's prattling.

"Some things are nonnegotiable," Stezak replied.

"You become a pillar of moral rectitude only when it comes to me?"

"Who said anything about morality?" he said.

We crossed Divisadero Street and approached the Panhandle. Golden Gate Park was less than a mile away.

"Those Niners sure are bad!" Yuri shouted.

"Would you shut up about the Niners already," I said.

Yuri caught my eye and looked down at his uncharacteristically buckled seat belt. I let out a soft chuckle as we passed Stanyan and entered the park.

"Yeah, those Niners are terrible," I said, recalling Yuri's confusion at one of our poker games over the term "buckle up" in describing the Niners' disappointing season.

Yuri sped up the cab.

"Slow down," Stezak said. "We're turning right up ahead."

Yuri stepped harder on the accelerator and I snapped on my seat belt. "You ready?" Yuri asked.

"Do it," I said.

Yuri jerked the car hard right and Stezak slammed into the driver's side door. Before Stezak could get his bearings, Yuri hit the gas and veered left, then right again, Stezak flying back and forth with every change of direction. Yuri bounced over the curb and headed straight for the trees. He glanced at me and I nodded my head, closing my eyes.

I heard the scrape of bushes and limbs on the cab and a couple of hard knocks from smaller trees. Then I heard Stezak yell, "Stop the car!" and a gunshot right as the cab slammed to a halt.

After a short bout of unconsciousness, I opened my eyes. Nobody was moving. Yuri was slumped over, moaning, and holding his neck. I leaned forward, but my shoulder, restrained by the seatbelt, remained four inches behind, well out of its socket.

Somehow, Yuri's kamikaze plan had worked. While we were banged up, Stezak's condition was far worse. He'd flown over the back seat and smashed into the dashboard. He was unconscious, his head and face bleeding, his left elbow turned the wrong direction. I grabbed the gun out of his right hand, cracked the door, and dropped it on the ground. The bullet had fired through the front window, missing Yuri by inches.

Yuri opened his door and fell out. I helped him up with my one good arm and we carried Stezak deeper into the woods. His breathing was light and slow. I made his odds of surviving fifty-fifty.

We hustled back to the cab and drove out of the park as inconspicuously as we could, a difficult task given the condition of the taxi. Yuri crisscrossed the city on side streets, the car sputtering and smoking the entire way, until we reached Wethersby's apartment.

"I'm sorry about this, Yuri," I said. "I don't have any money to pay for the repairs right now. Can you give me a couple of months?"

"Don't worry," he said. "I was thinking of quitting the taxi profession, anyway."

"What will you do?"

"Who knows? Something better. Maybe computers. Anything is possible. This is America."

"Spoken like a true immigrant," I said. "I need one more favor."

"Yes?"

"My shoulder. I need you to pop it back into socket."

"This will hurt," he said.

"I know."

I don't know how Yuri knew how to perform this medical procedure and I didn't ask. All I know is that one minute I was doing a shot of Johnnie and lying on the apartment floor, screaming in agony, and the next minute it was morning and my shoulder was sore, but intact, all because of my crazy, commie, cab driver buddy. Maybe there was hope for the world yet.

50

Saturday, November 4ᵗʰ, 5 p.m.

The big leagues were proving tougher than I'd assumed.

Unless I'd lucked out and Stezak had died in those woods. Then all I'd have to worry about is dodging a murder charge. Better than tangling with Stezak again. At least the justice system was supposed to administer justice blindly.

I decided I wouldn't make any plans about my situation until I heard of Stezak's fate. This plan also allowed me to enjoy the night's festivities untroubled. Tonight, once again, was fight night. Stezak or no Stezak, I was going to watch Alfredo box.

Fight night also meant it was time to add to Nelson's kitty. We were halfway to our goal. This was good in that we had $1,000; it was bad because we had one week left before our deadline was up and Bill put the records back on the floor. If I had to take one big swing, why not take it on Alfredo, the closest thing I knew to a sure thing?

Assuming the line and the limit were the same as for the last fight, I would have to bet differently this time if I wanted any real payback. I was thinking of sprinkling a straight win bet with a couple of wagers predicting which round the fight would end.

Dmitri put down his Abraham Lincoln biography and took off his glasses. "Did you know Abe had a great sense of humor?"

"I never heard that."

"Neither had I," he said, as if this was the most remarkable piece of information he'd ever come across.

"What are the odds on a first round KO?" I asked.

"Two to one for each one of the first two rounds. Five to one after that."

"How do you sleep at night making these ridiculous lines? Forget I asked. Give me two hundred on the third and fourth rounds, and two hundred on Alfredo to win. What's the line, minus a thousand?"

"Minus five hundred, and I upped the limit to three hundred," Dmitri answered.

"Minus five hundred? Really?" Those weren't good odds. They were incredible. Virgil couldn't beat him once out of fifty times, much less one out of five.

"Satterfield is getting some action on the other side," Dmitri explained.

"Then give me three-hundred on Alfredo straight and two-hundred on the third and fourth rounds."

"Done," Dmitri said, irritated.

"Hey, it's not my fault someone is giving money away to Marvin," I said.

"No, I guess it isn't."

Even better news than the line on the fight was that I didn't have to drive anywhere with Hammersmith and suffer his terrible musical taste again. Tonight was Alfredo's homecoming at the San Francisco Civic Center. Three thousand people packed the place, including luminaries such as Governor Brown, Supervisor Dan White, and the profoundly overrated Carlos Santana.

Hammersmith and I watched Kerry Mullins dismantle Shawn Green.

"That's another hundred dollars for the record fund," I said.

"Too bad you can't use that skill of yours to make some real money," Hammersmith said.

"Was that a compliment or a criticism?"

"Both, I guess. You hear about Stezak?" Hammersmith asked.

"No. What happened?"

Be dead. Be dead. Be dead.

"Got in some mysterious car wreck. He's laid up in the hospital."

"Is he gonna live?"

"Yeah. Broken arm. Broken nose. Concussion. But he'll live."

"That's too bad," I said.

Really, really, really too bad.

I was contemplating telling Hammersmith what happened when Don Stewart came out of the dressing room and tugged on my sleeve.

"Alfredo wants to talk to you," he said.

"Me?" It was less than an hour before the fight.

"Yeah."

I traded confused looks with Hammersmith and followed Don back into the locker room. Billy and Ricky were chatting while Alfredo loosened up in the corner.

"Hey, Alfredo. How you feeling?" I put up my hands, play fighting. He bobbed and air punched me four times in the ribs before it even registered with me.

He put his arm around my shoulder. "You still friends with that cop?" he asked.

"Not anymore. Why?"

"Damn. I need to talk to him."

"How about someone from the district attorney's office? I'm sitting with him tonight."

"Okay, good. I want to meet with him after the fight," Alfredo said.

"About what?"

"It's about that hooker who got killed."

"What about?" I was having flashes of doubt, the necklace still nagging at me.

"I think I know who it was."

"Yeah?"

"Yeah," he said.

"Yo, Alfredo!" Billy yelled. "We gotta tape you up."

"Okay," I said. "I'll bring the A.D.A. back after the fight."

"Thanks, man. See you later." Alfredo shadowboxed his way over to Billy.

I went back to my seat and relayed the news to Hammersmith.

"What could he know about Cindy?" Hammersmith asked.

"Beats me," I said.

We watched the rest of the undercard while nipping from my flask. An hour later, Alfredo emerged for the main event. He looked the same as the last fight. Playful, alert, and confident.

Virgil, on the other hand, looked serious. He was older

219

and more experienced than Alfredo's last opponent, and consequently less afraid. He was one of Pete Castillo's handful of real fighters, having fought more than thirty amateur fights, winning sixteen of them. Despite this decent pedigree, he was still too slow to keep up with Alfredo.

Like the last fight, Alfredo attacked from the jump. Virgil was prepared and covered up in the middle of the ring, clutching him. Being as strong as Alfredo, he pushed him off. He continued to avoid Alfredo's combinations, but he wasn't throwing any punches back. Alfredo stung him with a right at the end of the round. This fight wouldn't end in the first round, but it wasn't going to last more than five, either.

They went back to their corners. Alfredo's demeanor was calm, Ricky's even more nervous than usual. Virgil was taking long, deep breaths, listening to Pete's instructions.

The bell rang and again Alfredo pounced. Virgil, again, fought off the initial flurry. He stuck Alfredo with one solid body shot that caught Alfredo's attention. The round ended decisively for Alfredo. By my count, Alfredo had landed fifteen punches to Virgil's three.

Round three started and Virgil came out attacking. He threw a couple of jabs and danced around a little. Surprised he had lasted this long, Virgil now considered himself Alfredo's equal. This misplaced confidence would be his undoing.

"Alfredo ends it here," I told Hammersmith. "Ward will make a mistake."

Alfredo noticed Virgil was no longer covering up, sensed his opportunity. He bobbed his way close and hurt Virgil with a flurry of body shots. Then Alfredo spun out, low, like they'd been working on, and went right back with a combination to the head. Ward was out of his depth trying to box with Alfredo. I was counting my third round KO money already. Alfredo continued this line of attack, bobbing his way close, attacking the body, then breaking, only to reengage with shots to the head. I noticed his third approach, while effective, was a little sloppy. Alfredo stood up a little coming out of his turn and lowered his hands a touch.

The next time he attacked, Ward was prepared. Alfredo stood up a little straighter, his hands lowered a little further down. Virgil threw a sharp, square punch to Alfredo's jaw. This punch did more than surprise Alfredo. It sent him tumbling to the canvas, like a tree cut down by lightning.

Alfredo lay motionless. Ricky and Billy ran into the ring and surrounded him. Slops put smelling salt under Alfredo's nose to no effect.

Virgil had a confused look on his face while Pete hustled him to the locker room before the crowd turned against them both. The entire audience stood silent for fifteen minutes, until Alfredo was carried out on a stretcher.

51

Sunday, November 5th, 1 a.m.

The hospital was crowded with a mish mash of Alfredo's relatives, many of whom had resurfaced after being absent his entire life, the boys from Newman's, and Eddy Muller, the *Examiner's* boxing reporter.

I sat down next to Billy on a bench down the hall apart from the crowd.

"What's the deal?" I asked.

"He's unconscious."

"From one punch?"

"Doc says all it takes is one, so long as it's the right punch," Billy said.

"How long's he gonna be out?"

"Could be a day, could be forever."

"How's that possible?" I asked.

"I didn't go to medical school, Sleeper."

No, he didn't, and all the doctors and their medical degrees were worthless to me if they couldn't wake Alfredo from a coma after one punch from Virgil Ward. I don't care if it was the right punch or not. They had to wake him up.

If not for Alfredo's sake, then for mine.

"*When* he wakes up," I said, "you think he can get back to his old self?" I asked.

"Odds are against it. If there aren't any lingering physical effects, there will be psychological ones. Like a horse who gets spooked. They're never the same."

"What else?" I could tell something more was bothering him.

"I'm giving the gym to Don," he said.

"Giving it?"

"I've had enough."

"The place won't be the same without you. The Tenderloin won't be the same without you."

"The Tenderloin will be exactly the same," he said.

"Have it your way, you bastard. Nobody will miss you at all."

"I won't miss it, either," he said.

I waited for that Irish smile to curl, but it remained buried beneath the wrinkles of his weary, ashen face.

I wandered back to the Crescent around 2 a.m., needing Nelson's consoling more than the safety of Wethersby's apartment.

"I heard," Nelson said, as he awoke from dozing on the couch, waiting up for me no doubt. "You okay?"

"Nope," I said. We sat for a solid ten minutes in silence. "At least we have enough to buy most of your records back," I said.

"How's that?"

"I put down two-hundred on a third round KO at five to one. Subtract the other bets I lost and we netted another five hundred."

"It doesn't matter who KO'd who?"

"Nope," I said.

"Doesn't feel right to win it this way," Nelson said.

"Money doesn't care about right or wrong."

"I do," Nelson said.

He passed me his pipe and we sat on opposite ends of the couch without another word until we both fell asleep with Nicolette Larson singing "Lotta Love" softly in the background.

I woke up a few hours later. Despite my fatigue, soreness, and despondency, I mustered the energy to give the Crescent a quick once over. While sweeping the third floor hallway, dust filtering the gray morning light, I grasped the full gravity of my circumstances. If I didn't figure out a way to neutralize Stezak, and soon, I would have to leave town for good. Stezak would not let me live once he was out of the hospital. That was not speculation. That was a certainty.

After I'd gotten the Crescent into passable shape, I packed up some clothes and a couple of books for my return to the security of Wethersby's apartment. As I climbed down the front steps, I heard a car engine pop. At the same time, I noticed my building spontaneously self-combusting. First, a chunk of the stairwell exploded, followed by a piece of the cement wall.

I dove to the ground. That was no car engine popping and the holes in my building were not appearing randomly. Somebody was shooting at me. Another bullet shattered the small window on the front door. I heard car wheels screech. I raised my head in time to see the back of a yellow

Oldsmobile turning west on Eddy.

I scrambled down the stairs and slunk north to California Street. I called Janks from Wethersby's apartment.

"Janks. It's Sleeper. You ever find where Christano is?"

"Yeah. I've been calling you all day. He's in Sacramento."

"No, he's not. He's here," I said.

"Why do you say that?"

"Because he just tried to shoot me again."

"Shit. You okay?"

"I'm fine. You got an address for him in Sacramento?" I asked.

"Yeah."

"Wait a second while I get a pen," I said.

"No need. I'm going with you."

"What?" I asked.

"I got you into this mess. I'm gonna help get you out."

"I can't let you do that."

"Then I'm not giving you the address," Janks said.

Damn it. I was much more comfortable in a world where I was free to dislike Curtis Janko. I didn't appreciate him complicating matters with his decency.

"Pick me up at the Hyde Out tomorrow at ten," I said. "And bring two guns with you."

"What are you going to do?"

"Shoot Christano before he shoots me," I said.

52

Janks and I drove to Sacramento with two untraceable handguns he'd scrounged up. Not too difficult a task for a gunrunner, I thought. We didn't say much during the drive. The prospect of killing someone, a little outside our comfort zones, weighed on our minds. We were old hippies for chrissakes. Our conversation defaulted to former friends and acquaintances I'd lost contact with, which was basically everyone.

"Shelly?" I asked.

"Overdose."

"Bruce?"

"Lawyer."

"Nick?"

"Growing weed in Chico."

"Shirley?"

"Groupie."

"Albert?"

"Black Panther."

"Well, we'll always have Diamond Dan," I said.

The problem for the hippie diaspora for the last few years was defining who the enemy was. Back then it was simple. The war, Nixon, and The Man. What was left of the old countercultural hippie movement had splintered into dozens of smaller factions fighting individual battles. The environment, women's rights, gay rights, apartheid, socialism, you name it.

There was another group of leftovers: the ones who fell through the cracks, who didn't fit in anywhere anymore, except on the margin. It was a vast, unruly group, large enough to include both Janks and myself.

After finding Christano's place, we knew we had to come up with another plan. Christano lived on the top floor of a three-story walk-up. If we tried to break in, Christano would have the jump on us.

We waited outside his apartment for another tense hour until he emerged around 11:30 p.m.

"Perfect, I said. "He's going to his local."

"How can you tell?" Janks asked.

"Trust me," I said.

We followed him on foot for a few blocks until he stopped at a bar called Joe Marty's.

"Good call, Sleeper," Janks said.

"Bars are my one area of expertise," I said. "I can't go inside. He'll recognize me. Go in and check it out. See if there's a back entrance."

"Where are you gonna be?"

"Over there." I pointed to a pub across the street.

"Okay," Janks said, never one to shy away from a fight.

I secured a window table at the opposing bar and waited for Janks to return.

He joined me a few minutes later. "It's good," he said. "There's no back door. We can wait here and follow him home."

We nervously watched the bar across street until closing, fortifying our courage with beer and whiskey.

"Something's bothering me," I said.

"What's that?"

"I didn't see a yellow Olds parked anywhere, did you?"

"Probably parked it in his garage."

"Could be."

Two more scotches and too much small talk later, Christano stumbled out alone at closing. I could tell from his gate that he'd had his fill and then some. I closed my eyes to make sure I was ready to go through with this. The alternatives were go to the police or wait for him to shoot me again. Neither sounded promising.

When I opened my eyes, Janks was waiting for my decision.

"Well?" he asked.

"Let's do it."

We hurried out the door, followed Christano from a good distance. There was no reason to get too close. We knew his destination. Or so we thought. He turned unexpectedly onto a side street a block before his place. We hurried around the corner. He was gone. We looked at each other, bewildered.

Then we heard a click.

"Hands up where I can see them," Christano said, apparently not as inebriated as I'd thought. He patted us down, grabbed both guns from our pockets, and dumped the bullets on the sidewalk. "Now turn around," he said.

"Hi, Sniffles," I said.

"Oh, Jesus, this oughta be good. What the fuck you doing

here?" he asked. "You come back for revenge or something?"

"I'm not a spiteful guy. I came back in self-defense."

"Why would you need to do that?"

"Oh, come on," Janks spluttered.

"Who the hell are you?"

"I'm the one who got Sleeper into this trouble."

"What are you talking about?" Christano asked.

"I'm the one who told Jones about Sleeper," Janks said.

"Who's Jones?"

"The guy who hired you to shoot him," Janks said. "Jim Jones."

"He didn't hire me to shoot him."

Janks and I looked at each other, confused.

"Was it Urbancyck?" I asked.

"It wasn't anybody."

"Nobody hired you to shoot me?"

"Why would anyone want *you* dead?" Christano said.

"Then why did you do it?"

"Because you're annoying. You got a smart mouth. Believe me, if this was a hired job I wouldn't have played poker with you in the first place, and you for sure wouldn't still be breathing."

I wanted to grab Christano's gun and turn it on Janks for getting us into this fix.

"So what am I supposed to do with you now?" Christano asked.

"Look, the reason we're here is we thought you had some unfinished business with me. If that's not the case, I got no beef with you," I said. "I don't suppose a simple 'sorry' would suffice?"

He laughed, but didn't lower his gun. He looked back and

forth at the apartment buildings on both sides of the street. A handful of lights were on. "Shit," he mumbled. Those night owls saved our lives; too many potential witnesses for a professional like Christano.

"Take off your clothes," he said.

"What?" I asked.

"You heard me," he said. "Strip or I shoot. You can leave your underwear on. Nobody wants to see those little things between your legs."

I saw Janks kicking off his shoes out of the corner of my eye.

"What's the point?" I asked.

"What's the point of embarrassing someone in a friendly poker game?" he said. "Now get on with it." I dutifully disrobed, cursing Janks with every garment that hit the sidewalk. "Now start running. If I ever see either of you back in Sacramento I'll assume you're here to shoot me and I'll shoot you first. Got it?"

"Got it," I said through clenched teeth.

Back in Janks's car, I let him have it. "You almost got us killed for no reason. Why'd you think Jones hired him again?"

"That's what I thought she said. I must have misinterpreted her."

"Not hard to believe," I said.

"Don't talk to me like that. I had your back in a big way."

"I'll watch my own back from now on. It's safer."

"Helping you is a thankless job, anyway," Janks said.

"You want a thank you? Thanks for almost getting us shot."

"Fuck off, Sleeper."

"Same to you, Janks."

Back to being enemies, and the world could resume spinning smoothly on its axis.

We drove back to San Francisco in our tighty-whities in 75 minutes flat. I leaned against the car window and stared vacantly at the dark, rolling hills of Vallejo, unsettled by the fact that Christano had shot me not for something I had done, but for simply being myself. Even more troubling was the fact that someone was still out there, driving a yellow Olds, circling my block, waiting for another opportunity to try again.

53

Thursday, November 9th, 2 p.m.

Just because the Temple hadn't hired Christano to shoot me didn't mean they were exonerated of any wrongdoing, including the most recent attempt on my life. I knew about the Temple's gunrunning, Cindy's murder, and the election fraud, any one of which would make me their target. And as Lady Ellinger could confirm, they already knew where I lived.

Mazor was my way into the Temple. I knew he was pulling something on the Concerned Relatives, even if I didn't know exactly what. I enlisted Jeannie, again, in a plan to smoke Mazor out. She would bring him a new, fictional file for his safekeeping. I would then follow Mazor to find out what, if anything, he was doing with their information.

Jeannie dropped off the dummy file while I waited outside the Russ Parking Garage in the backseat of a cab Yuri borrowed from a friend. Ten minutes after Jeannie left the building, Mazor exited in his red convertible. Not exactly the type of car you'd want your private detective to drive.

Mazor drove west on Pine, cut south on Gough, then

west again on Geary. My pulse raced as I anticipated his destination. I knew I would have to confront someone at the Temple eventually. I didn't know it would be now, and right in the belly of the beast.

Mazor double parked in front of the Peoples Temple on Geary at Fillmore. Yuri dropped me on the opposite side of the street, and I walked west, situating myself on the bridge crossing Geary at Steiner. From this vantage point I could see the entire block, starting with the original Fillmore Auditorium, now a Nation of Islam Temple, followed by another music hall, 1839, and then the Temple at 1859 Geary Street.

With three arching doorways below three large matching windows, the light brick building looked like a cross between a library and a YMCA. A small, inconspicuous, six-by-four-foot sign, reminiscent to that of a liquor store, jutted out from the second floor, with "Peoples Temple" written in red block letters.

Apart from the higher-ups in the Temple who used the building as their headquarters when back in the States, there hadn't been much activity here since the Temples move to Guyana. What remained behind was a skeleton crew, enough to maintain the building and a semblance of a neighborhood presence. It also housed the feral woman who'd gnawed on my finger, tied up Lady Ellinger, and stolen Cindy's files.

The wind whipped down Geary Street and I smoked another cigarette to keep warm. The front door of the Temple was propped open, another pretense of being a place of worship like any other, where people were free to come and go as they pleased.

I waited until Mazor exited, then crossed the bridge and entered the Temple from the west. Inside was an empty foyer that fed you into a large nondescript banquet room resembling a VFW hall. I ascended a set of *Gone With The Wind* stairs into a larger auditorium where they held their services. Behind me was a large balcony, in front the stage where Jones preached.

Behind the stage were two sets of stairs. One led to Jones's office, the other to a dormitory housing a handful of Temple members.

The door leading to Jones's office was locked. I tried the one to residence. It clicked open and I tiptoed to the top and a long, narrow hallway. I held my breath and listened for the sound of human activity. Nothing. I opened all seven of the unlocked bedroom doors and found them stripped bare.

There was a utility closet next to the bathroom. I remembered Wanda saying that the Angels' enforcer, my female attacker, slept in a closet. I assumed Wanda was speaking figuratively, not literally. I pushed open the closet door. Wanda had meant precisely what she'd said.

A towel-sized mat lay on the floor surround by a handful of folded clothes, a glass, a toothbrush, a Bible, some newspapers, and a stack of folders. One of the folder wasn't hers, though. The bright red one that matched all of Cindy's other Jim Jones files.

"Who are you?" The voice was behind me.

I whirled around to find my lupine adversary standing in the closet doorway, narrowing her yellow eyes at me. My finger throbbed at the memory of our last encounter. "I'm Joe's driver," I stammered. "He thought he left a file behind."

"Joe didn't forget any folders," she said.

"He must have been mistaken."

"You don't work for Joe. What do you want?"

I dropped the act. "I want to know why you have Cindy Teague's file here."

"Excuse me?"

"You heard me. That bright red one there. That was Cindy's."

"That is Temple property. She stole it."

"And Mazor returned it to you," I said.

She moved in front of the narrow doorway. "Who are you?" she asked.

"Did you kill Cindy Teague?" I responded.

"That treasonous whore got what she deserved."

"You are one crazy bitch," I said.

Unsurprisingly, that set her crazy-ass off. She hurled herself onto me, wrapping her legs around my waist like a girlfriend welcoming home her boyfriend from war, while head-butting me in the middle of my forehead. My head snapped backwards and I was blinded by sparkling red and orange lights.

I regained my sight in time for her to hop down and knee me in the groin. As I fell over, I reached out and took her down with me. Size appeared to be my only advantage in this matchup.

I landed on top of her, my right shoulder colliding with her solar plexus. She gasped and flailed, the wind knocked out of her. She caught her breath and pushed my head backwards, digging her ring finger into my left eye.

I grabbed her wrist and pried her finger out of my eye before it pushed its way to my optic nerve. She used this reprieve to wriggle free and roll onto her bed, pulling a gun from under the pillow. She jumped onto one knee and cocked the pistol. I dove out of the doorway as she fired. The bullet tore through the wall behind me.

I jumped to my feet and we crashed into one another as she ran out of her closet. The gun fell to the floor and we dove for it, like it was a football fumbled at the goal line.

I slowly began to gain control of the gun. Having been bitten and head-butted by her, I anticipated either move by palming her chin and shoving her head away from me. She thrashed and kicked. One of her knees banged the gun and it loosened from our grip. We retightened our grasps simultaneously and one of us squeezed the trigger.

The gun fired a hot, deafening blast.

I took inventory of myself. No new holes anywhere on my body. But judging by the way my adversary had stopped struggling, I didn't think she could say the same. She rolled onto her back, her white t-shirt rapidly transforming into a red tie-dye.

"Help me," she said. "Please, go get help."

I couldn't care less if she died. In fact, that was my preference. But I needed her alive if I wanted to prove the Temple's involvement in Cindy's and George's deaths.

I hopped down the stairs three at a time out to Geary Street. Cops are like bars when you crave a drink, there's never one around when you need one. I ran across the street to Jack's and asked to make a call. The bartender stared at my bloodstained shirt, and handed me the phone from underneath the bar. While I dialed the operator and requested an ambulance, he put a shot of tequila in front of me. I slammed it down in one throat-ripping gulp.

I ran back across the street and into the Temple. I was

halfway to the second floor when I noticed a new decorative detail on the staircase: a red streak of blood right down the middle. I followed the stripe back down the stairs, through the hallway, and out the rear door. It stopped in the middle of the alley, where a car must have been parked before my attacker climbed in and drove off.

I heard sirens approaching. I sprinted back up to her closet to retrieve Cindy's file. It was gone, as were most of the others. I snatched the remaining two files and sprinted back down the stairs. Wary of running into either the EMTs or Temple security, I pried open a window on the landing and climbed up the fire escape to the roof. I hopped to the music club next door and continued down the block on the rooftops, descending down the fire escape of the old Fillmore Auditorium.

Just when I thought this day couldn't get any weirder, I stopped a few blocks down Fillmore Street to look at the folders I'd taken. The thicker one was titled, "Letters to Dad." I couldn't imagine what that folder contained and I'm glad I didn't read it until I was home with a drink in my hand. The contents were more twisted than anything I could have conjured on my own.

54

Thursday, November 9th, 4 p.m.

An hour later, I called Jeannie from Wethersby's apartment.

"I was right. Mazor's double crossing you," I said.

"What?" she asked.

"This is Sleeper. Mazor. He's giving your files to the Temple."

"Damnit. I didn't want to believe you. Why would he do that?" she asked.

"I don't know, but he is. I followed him to the Temple and saw one of Cindy's files on Jones there."

"Are you sure?"

"I'm positive."

"You know what this means, don't you? We're all in much more danger than we thought," she said.

"You need to tell the rest of the Concerned Relatives," I said.

"Okay, okay. Thanks, Sleeper."

The relief I felt from warning Jeannie lasted only as long as it took me to open the 'Letters to Dad' file I'd stolen from the Temple. I read its contents on my recliner, at first with trepidation, then with alarm, and finally in horror. "Dad" turned out to be Jim Jones, and the letters were from members vowing to take revenge on the Temples' enemies. I read the dozen or so missives, my stomach tightening another notch with every one:

Dad –

I would like to go back and get Liz Forman and Lester Kingsolving. McElvane agreed with me one time that I would be capable of assassination and maybe get by with it. After it was done I would commit self-immolation at an appropriate location.

****

Dear Dad

I am again willing to go & get our enemies. I will make sure that each time I get one, I will be ready to blow myself up. They also would look like accidents. Starting with Tim.

****

Dad,

I feel it would be most effective and demoralizing to our enemies if one of the key traitors would disappear totally and without a trace. This could be accomplished with a few people, a rented van, and some rugs like the "Tupamaros" did in the film we saw. Just come up behind, blackjack him, wrap him in a rug and drive off.

Another approach along the same line would be to get an ambulance, some white uniforms and either blackjack him or manhandle him into a straight jacket and give him a quick sedative. People who witness the pick up are less likely to question or interfere if they think we're just picking up another "loony."

I am willing to volunteer to assassinate as many traitors as possible by rifle or poison or any other means and to commit revolutionary suicide before apprehension. I feel with a little training I would stand a good chance to get one or two before removing myself. If I could get to a conference of traitors I could detonate myself in their midst and get rid of more.

Thank you Dad

****

Dad,

Here is my plan to get Grace or the Myrtles. Let about 4 people seem as if they were run out of the Temple and here is the way one of the people could call from the Port of Spain say we need help to get to Miami and tell them to send plane fare for 4 people, tell them we are willing to talk about it here. But it will have to be in the work for about 3 months here and in Georgetown, and you and the people say we had stole some money and our passport. Dad, there is much more I have in my head I would pass on to the office and not to the whole family because some of the things that happen here seem to get back there.

****

To Dad:

Tim Stone is the #1 cause of this. I believe if a number of our security (four or six) but first, delay the conference since

the meeting is tomorrow and get another date for this confer-
ence. Get our security to pinpoint Tim Stone at the conference
or before the conference and use him for bargaining power or
hold him as a ace card to determine our maneuvers to protect
our cause of what we stand for. I know this is kidnapping but
right now we are at a do or die matter. We have to stop this
madness of all these lies and holding up our shipments to
protect our name of Peoples Temple.

****

Dad,
I am a senior and I am willing to go and fight for this cause,
and also do my husband in. My life has no purpose but live
for socialism, and I am willing to give up my life so socialism
will live on.

I closed the file and walked directly to the corner store in
my bare feet. I returned with a pint of Johnnie Red and
locked myself in the apartment. I reacted to these letters the
only way any sentient being should have. I got blind drunk.

55

As disturbing as those letters were to me, and as frightening as they would be to Grace, Tim, and the Mills—formerly the Myrtles—I hoped they would also constitute enough evidence to approach Maguire again without sounding like a raving lunatic. After much begging and cajoling on my part, Maguire relented, agreeing to meet me at Mama's during his fifteen-minute lunch break.

"Alright, lay it out for me," he said, tersely, in between bites of his French Dip sandwich and gulps of coffee.

"I've got the whole thing pieced together. See if this works for you: Cindy tries to use Prokes's notebook detailing the Moscone deal to get her sister back. She gives it to Mazor, who is supposed to be doing the negotiating with Jones, only Mazor double crosses Cindy, and Jones has her killed."

Maguire stopped chewing. "Gotta admit, it fits," he said.

"But it gets better. Or worse."

"How's that?"

"It also explains George Urbancyck's murder. George knows about Prokes's file from Cindy, but instead of using

242

it to negotiate with Jones, like Cindy was planning, George uses it to roll on Moscone with the Feds."

"I thought you said Mazor had the file?"

"Mazor did have it, but George was gonna get it back from Mazor the night he died. Or at least that's what George thought. But George gets shot on his way to the meet. This happens the night before he's supposed to testify. You don't find all of this strange?"

Maguire leaned back in his chair and threw his napkin on his plate. "Goddamn, Hayes. I think, these whacko assassination letters are enough."

"Enough for what?"

"Enough evidence for a warrant to get us in the Temple."

"I don't think you'll find the woman."

"Fuck her. I hope she bled out. I want Jones."

"Hurry up, before one of his other lunatic children finishes me off."

"Lunch is on me," he said.

"You're damn right it is."

After my meeting with Maguire, my spirits bolstered a bit for the first time in weeks, Andre, Billy's gopher, ran me down on Larkin Street.

"Sleeper, wait up."

"Hey, Andre."

"Where you been? Billy's been looking for you."

"What's going on?"

"Come down to the hospital," he said, and followed that request with the three greatest words I'd ever heard. "Alfredo woke up."

One lung or not, I jogged as far as I could, about a block

and a half, before settling into a brisk walk. In between coughing fits, my mind raced back and forth from Alfredo to Jones, the best and the worst the world had to offer.

Alfredo was propped up in his hospital bed, his eyes struggling to stay open. The tube was out of his mouth. He looked about how I looked after a rough night of drinking, neither healthy nor terminal. Billy and Ricky were there, as well as a hot little number I'd never seen before. Even in a coma, Alfredo had game.

"Hey, buddy," I said.

Alfredo curved his lips into something resembling a smile.

"You gave us all a scare."

He nodded his head and whispered, "Sorry."

"You should be," I joked.

"Don't mind Sleeper," Billy said. "He's still mad that he lost money on you."

I couldn't tell Alfredo, or Billy, I'd actually made money on Alfredo's misfortune. "The only people who made money on that fight were the bookies," I said. Then it hit me. "Wait, that's not true. The bookies weren't the only ones."

"What do you mean?" Ricky asked.

"I think I figured out what's been bothering me about the fight."

56

Friday, November 10ᵗʰ, 4 p.m.

Like most days, the Acropolis was empty in mid-afternoon. Niko was behind the counter washing dishes. He nodded upstairs, indicating that Dmitri was up in his office.

I climbed the backstairs, breathing heavily, and knocked on the half-open door.

"Come in," Dmitri said, unconcerned about being caught with the stolen necklace he was appraising. Not the smartest idea, given the recent bust of a South of Market fencing operation.

"What's going on, Sleeper?"

"Dmitri," I said, shutting the door behind me.

Picking up on the import of the closed door, he put down his magnifying glass. "Whatsup?" he asked.

"I've been thinking about the Alfredo fight."

"I heard he woke up. Minor miracle, huh?"

"Pretty low bar for miracles," I said. "Listen, when I bet that fight with you, you upped my limit from two to three hundred dollars. You remember that?"

"Someone stepped up on Virgil's side. Five grand if I

remember right."

"That's what's bothering me."

"What's that?" he asked.

"Why somebody would step up on Virgil."

"What do you mean?"

"The action Satterfield was getting on Virgil, doesn't it seem a little fishy in hindsight?"

"I don't know. I've seen luckier," Dmitri said.

"When?"

Dmitri leaned back in his chair and studied me. "Nothing comes to mind," he said. "You're thinking the fight was fixed?"

"Seems like somebody knew something."

"That's one helluva dive Alfredo took, isn't it? To go into a coma," Dmitri said.

"That part doesn't make sense. But my gambling alarm is going off. You think you can talk to Marvin? See if he'll open up about who laid down the wood on Virgil?"

Dmitri tapped his fingers on his desk for so long I almost jumped over it and broke them one by one. "Okay," he said. "Marvin was bitchin' to me yesterday some guy hitting another boxing bet. Maybe it was the same guy."

Dmitri picked up the phone. "Marvin...Yeah. Hey, remember that guy who hit on the Pedro Fernandez fight... Yeah, that's the one. He come by to pick up his money yet?... No? You know his name?...How about what he looks like?... Okay, thanks...Yeah, I had someone who hit that fight, too. I wanted to see if it was the same guy. It wasn't...Alright. Bye."

He replaced the receiver and drummed the damn desk again with his stubby little digits.

"What did he say?" I asked.

246

"I can't decide if I want to tell you," Dmitri said.

"Why not?"

"Because I don't want you to do anything stupid."

"Stupid is in the eye of the beholder," I said.

"Precisely my concern. I'm telling you this for Alfredo and what he means to the T.L. The guy who made the bet is coming by today to pick up his money."

"Did he say what he looks like?"

"Said he looks like a grape picker."

"Mexican?"

"Said he looks right off the truck."

"Doesn't sound like a professional gambler, does it?"

"They come in all shapes and sizes." He gave me an accusatory look.

"Thanks, Dmitri."

"Sleeper?"

"Yeah?" I waited for Dmitri's usual paternalistic admonishment.

"Good luck."

57

Friday, November 10th, 5 p.m.

Having no idea when the pick-up was happening, I scurried west on Eddy Street as fast as I could. As I turned right onto Jones, I bumped dead into Sal, Cindy's pimp.

"What the fuck?" he said, before recognizing me. He stopped and glared. I prepared myself for another slashing. Instead he smirked and walked away.

"Hey," I said. "I'm right here. If you're gonna finish the job, go ahead. What are you waiting for?"

"What are you talking about?" he asked.

"The money I owe you for Lori. The thousand bucks. I don't have it."

"We're square, motherfucker."

"How's that?"

"You're off the hook."

"What?"

"Your crippled pal paid your tab. You didn't know?"

"Nelson paid you a thousand dollars. How—" *The record money, that's how.*

"If that's his name. You're a lucky man. I would have

enjoyed slicing you up," he said, and continued down Eddy.

He was right, I thought, as I sat down at Jonell's horse-shoe-shaped bar and ordered a Bud. Having a friend like Nelson was lucky. So much so, that it almost made up for everything else that was wrong with the world.

Satterfield sat across the bar studying the sports section in a tan leisure suit. His beard and receding afro were the same four inches in length. Unlike Dmitri, who never tipped a glass until after dinner, Satterfield sipped on Crown Royal throughout the day, never getting too high nor too low, like a steady I.V. drip keeping him properly medicated.

A couple of humps straggled in to place bets with Marvin, who never wrote anything down. I never saw Satterfield reach in his pocket to pay anyone off, either. What a business.

As I cracked my fourth beer, a twenty-something Mexican walked in and sat next to Satterfield. The guy was short, sported a mustache, and was dressed in Wranglers and a plaid shirt. He had to be Marvin's grape picker. He looked about as comfortable in a bar as I would in a vineyard.

Satterfield nodded to Kim, the bartender, who walked into the back room and returned with a paper bag. She handed it to Satterfield, who passed it on to the Mexican, making him, literally, the bagman.

In order to avoid suspicion, I finished my beer and walked outside before they concluded their business. As I passed behind them, Satterfield held the guy's arm, leaned in, and whispered something about where he should take his business next time. He sat back up and said, "Make sure you tell him that."

The bagman nodded, put the sack into his backpack, and followed me outside.

I thought the trail would end with the license plate number of whatever car he hopped inside. Confirming my suspicion that he wasn't a gambling mastermind, however, he walked down the street and waited for the 26 Valencia bus. I continued on to the next stop.

He wasn't the least concerned about being followed. Once on the bus, he even reached in the backpack to touch the money. We meandered through the Mission until he hopped off at Army and hoofed it east to Shotwell.

He reached his destination, a tiny bungalow house perched on an upslope, and climbed the flight of twenty stairs to the front door. My eyes drifted back down to the small carport below. Parked in the driveway was a bright yellow Oldsmobile.

The bagman knocked on the front door, and we both waited for the door to open. When Pete Castillo, Virgil Ward's trainer, emerged from inside, I almost coughed up my remaining lung. I guess we had all underestimated Pete this whole time; he wasn't so harmless after all.

I smoked a nail down the block, sussing out the details of Pete's scam. It took two more cigarettes to put it all together. When I did, I was disgusted by my blinkered take on the events of the last few months.

The bagman left twenty minutes later with, I was sure, no more than twenty dollars in his pocket for his efforts. I approached Pete's house, unarmed. Not the best idea given the shots that had been fired at me from his yellow Olds.

"Sleeper?" he said through the cracked door. At least I had the element of surprise.

"Can I come in?" I asked.

"Give me a second." He tried shutting the door, but I

stuck my foot in before it closed.

"Thanks," I said, letting myself into the saddest bachelor pad you'd ever seen. There was a ratty orange plaid couch next to a ratty green plaid chair. Situated between the chair and a small black and white television was a T.V. tray with a lone Tecate on top.

"Beer?" he offered.

"No."

Pete shrugged and flopped into his easy chair, still in his robe and pajamas. I lowered myself onto the couch next to him. "I heard Alfredo woke up," he said, glancing at me out of the corner of his eye.

"Yeah."

"*Gracias a Dios.*"

"You got anything you want to tell me about that fight?" I asked.

"Why would I?" he said.

"You're sure? Nothing at all?" I said.

"What's to say? Lucky punch."

"Someone didn't think it was so lucky," I said.

"What do you mean?" Pete sat up in his chair.

"Someone bet five grand with Marvin Satterfield that Virgil would win."

"They did?" Pete asked.

"Can we stop beating around the bush, Pete? I followed your bagman here. I know it was you."

Pete jumped out of his chair, no doubt to go for his gun. I was on top of him before he could reach his destination.

"Start talking, Pete." I had him pinned down and grabbed his shirt with both hands.

"Nothing wrong with backing your own boxer!" he shouted.

"Bullshit. You bet five thousand on Virgil. That's more than backing your boxer."

"He was training good, man. What the fuck?"

"Bullshit."

I lifted him up and slammed his head against the floor.

"I was lucky, I swear!" Pete yelled.

"What did you put in the gloves, Pete?" I yelled back.

"What?"

"What did you put in Virgil's gloves? There is no way one punch could do that much damage. No way." I grabbed his neck. "What did you put in the gloves?"

"Nada, man. I swear."

I bashed his head against the floor again. "Tell me goddamnit." I slammed his head again, this time hard enough that a small rivulet of blood raced across the floor.

"*Yeso de Paris!*" he screamed.

"What?"

"*Yeso de Paris.*" He caught his breath. "Plaster of Paris." He closed his eyes and whispered it once more. "Plaster of Paris."

I let go and walked back to the kitchen, returning with a dishrag full of ice and a Tecate. "Get up," I ordered.

Pete struggled to his feet and sat back down in his recliner. I handed him the makeshift ice bag and cracked the Tecate for myself. "It wasn't my idea," he whimpered.

"I know," I said. "I know."

"What else do you know?" Pete asked.

"Pretty much all of it. One question, though, Pete. How did Stezak find out you killed Cindy?"

"Kill Cindy? I didn't kill that girl."

252

"Then who did?" I asked, closing in on him as menacingly as I could.

"If he finds out I told you, I'm a dead man."

"As is, you're going to jail for a long time. If you tell me what happened, maybe I can help cut you a deal with the cops."

"You? How you gonna do that?" Pete asked.

"I'm the only option you got."

Pete shrugged and started talking. Thirty minutes later, after hearing all the despicable details, I called Hammersmith from Pete's house.

"You can thank me later," I told him, "because I'm about to make your career."

"Count me as dubious," he said.

"Trust me. This is front page material."

"Okay. I'll bite."

"Alfredo's fight was fixed and I have the fixer."

"Who's that?"

"Not so quick. You're going to have to do some work, too. Have Nelson let you into my apartment. All you have to do after that is hide in the bathroom and listen. I'll get the guy to confess to everything there."

"Don't yank my chain, Sleeper."

"I'm not. Oh, and bring a homicide cop, too."

"I thought you said this was about boxing?"

"It is. But as a little bonus, I'm bringing you the guy who killed Cindy, too."

"Tell me now if you're drunk, buddy," he said. "I won't be mad."

"I'm not drunk," I replied, "but I wish I was."

58

Friday, November 10ᵗʰ, 11 p.m.

Pete sat in another dilapidated easy chair, this one in my apartment, unaware that Hammersmith and a cop were squeezed into my bathroom.

The buzzer rang.

A minute later, I opened the door to Ricky, who reached for a hug, but stopped when he saw Pete. "What's he doing here?" Ricky asked.

"He's got something he wants to tell you," I said. "Sit down."

He crossed the room and sat on the folding chair I'd brought in from the laundry room. "So?" he said.

"Remember when I told you something was bothering me about the fight?" I started.

"Yeah," Ricky answered.

"Well, I figured it out. I hadn't thought much of it at the time, but someone laid down a decent-sized bet on Virgil."

"I'm not getting you," Ricky said.

"It didn't make sense. Why would anyone risk real money betting against Alfredo?"

"Depends on the odds, doesn't it?" Ricky answered.

"Even at long odds, there's nobody in the T.L. who could afford to take a flyer on Virgil for that size money. Twenty dollars, maybe. Possibly a hundred. But five thousand? I don't care what the odds are. That doesn't fit."

"Go on," Ricky said.

"The reason someone would bet that money was if they knew Alfredo would lose."

Ricky shot a glance at Pete, then asked, "How could anyone know that?"

"Somebody did," I said.

Ricky's eyes narrowed. He jumped out of his seat at Pete. I lunged in between them.

"Sit down, Ricky," I said. "I'm not done."

"Forget it. I'm leaving. I don't want to be in the same room with this *pendejo*," he said, pointing at Pete.

"Aren't you even a little curious to know how he knew?" I asked.

"I don't want to know. I might do something I'll regret."

"I don't think that's why," I said.

Ricky fixed his glare at me now. "No?"

"I don't think you're curious because I think you already know."

"What are you talking about, Sleeper?"

"Come on, the conditioning of the head. The neck strengthening, having heavyweights wail on Alfredo. You were trying to protect Alfredo, in your own delusional way."

"I'm his trainer. It's my job."

"No. You knew he was gonna get hit with cement, and you wanted him to survive it."

"You're crazy," he said. "I'm fucking leaving."

"I'll go to the police, Ricky."

He paused at the door, his back turned to me.

I continued, "Virgil was waiting on Alfredo to stand up coming out of his turn. He knew it was coming. He was sitting on it. How did he know Alfredo stood up? He'd never done it in a fight because Alfredo's fights never lasted that long. Alfredo only did it when he was training."

"Sleeper, why would I—"

"Because Stezak was squeezing you for money."

"Why would I owe—"

"Drop the fucking act! Don't make me spell it all out. Can't you tell by now that I know? I know you killed Cindy, and I know Stezak caught you."

He faced me, in a rage. I pulled Nelson's .22 from the small of my back. "Sit down, Ricky."

He stayed standing, his mouth twitching.

"Now," I said, pointing the gun at him.

He crossed the room and sat on the folding chair, his body tense and shaking. "You're crazy, man," he mumbled.

"No, I'm not, Ricky. And you know who else doesn't think so? Alfredo. He tried to tell me before the fight. Should we go down there together and have him finish the story?"

He looked at me stunned, his eyes begging for me to be lying about Alfredo knowing.

"Alfredo knows you killed Cindy," I continued. "He doesn't know about the fight. I don't think he suspects his own brother would set him up to be punched with cement gloves."

Ricky looked relieved, clearly caring more about Alfredo not knowing about the fixed fight than he did about murdering Cindy.

I pointed the gun at his forehead. "Start talking, Ricky," I said.

He looked around the room, trying to find a way out, resting his gaze on Pete.

"I didn't say nothing about nothing, man," Pete said. "I swear. He figured this shit out himself."

"Why do you say Alfredo knows about Cindy?" Ricky asked.

"My guess? The necklace," I said.

"What necklace?"

"The one Stezak returned to me. Alfredo's first communion necklace. Your mom gave you one, too, didn't she? That's the one Stezak had. But your necklace didn't come with a cross, it came with an angel. A little gold angel, right? The same one that rested on Cindy's dead body."

"How could you know about that?" Ricky asked.

"I should have figured it out sooner. A friend told me she saw someone who looked like Alfredo in a cop car outside Cindy's the night she was killed, and I dismissed it. Then I saw your crazy act in person with Mercedes."

"Mercedes had it coming. The little *puta*," he said.

"No she didn't, and you knew that then. Last, there was Stezak. He's been focused on squeezing Alfredo since day one. For his scheme to work, he had to be certain that the other suspects, George, Jones, whoever—were innocent. If they were busted before Alfredo took his fall, his game would be up. He knew they were innocent because he knew it was you. How did Stezak find out, Ricky?"

"Fuck you, Sleeper. We're leaving. Call the cops if you want. They can't touch us. Stezak will make sure of that."

"Too late. We already called the cops and Pete cut a deal.

Stezak can't save you now."

"You stupid, fucking idiot." He jumped on Pete before I could react. I turned my gun around and hit him on the side of the head. A gash the width of a ruler opened up under his thick, black hair.

"Stay where you are," I yelled, more for Hammersmith than for Ricky. I picked him up with one hand and sat him back down. "Now, how did Stezak find out?"

He stared at me, biting his lip so hard I thought it would burst. I pointed the gun and cocked it. He studied the gun, trying to decide if taking a bullet right now might be the best option for his predicament.

"Porto. His fat flunky. He was a customer of Cindy's, too. He barged in when he heard me and Cindy fighting."

"Fighting? That's what you call it? Jesus, Ricky. Then what, he and Stezak squeezed you for money?"

"Yeah," Ricky said, his hands on top of his head.

"So you and Stezak conspire to have Alfredo throw a fight. You didn't want Alfredo to know you were behind it, so you had Stezak do the dirty work. When Alfredo comes to you for advice, you'd tell him to go down. But I screwed things up when I showed up at Newman's while Stezak and Porto were working over Alfredo. Then I completely derailed your plan by getting Stezak off Alfredo's back by giving him valuable information about the FBI investigating him."

"You should have stayed out of it," Ricky said.

"You knew I wouldn't stop once I started. That's why you had Pete shoot off a few rounds at me."

"I was only trying to scare you, Sleeper, I swear," Pete said.

"The problem is you still owed Stezak the money," I said to Ricky, "with no way of paying it back."

"You don't understand. Stezak said he was going to throw Alfredo in jail for real. I didn't have a choice. I couldn't let him do that to Fredo."

"So you cut Pete in on your plan," I said.

Ricky returned his hands to his head. "Yeah," he whimpered, "that's everything. Almost."

"Almost?" I asked.

"You think you're so goddamn smart," Ricky snarled. "But you got one thing wrong. I didn't kill Cindy."

"Bullshit. None of the rest makes sense without the underlying crime."

"What if the cops set me up?"

"I don't believe you. Why would they do that?" I asked.

"I don't know, man. Cindy and I got in a fight. That's it. We had a date and she cancelled it. Said she had some meeting." *The meeting with the reporter*, I remembered. "So we got into it, pretty bad. We hit each other and yes, I choked her. That's when Porto showed up looking for some action from Cindy, too. So me and him go at it a little. Until he pulls his gun on me. Then he takes me outside and squeezes me for a grand."

"Just a grand?"

"Yeah. Until the next day. Then he and Stezak show up at the gym and tell me Cindy's dead. They say now the price is fifty large. Said that's the going rate for beating a murder rap."

I wasn't buying it, even if Ricky's story confirmed what I already suspected about Porto's presence in the Triangle that night.

"So who killed Cindy?" I asked. "Porto? I don't think so. I might believe it if you said Stezak. But Porto, he's fat and dumb. Not evil."

"I don't know who killed her. I only know I didn't. She was alive when I left. But I had no choice but to go along. They had my fingerprints on her neck and the gold angel I'd given her as a gift. It didn't matter whether I did it or not."

And it didn't matter to me if he was lying or not. Hammersmith had heard everything and now it would be up to him to sort it out. The one thing Ricky couldn't lie his way out of was setting up Alfredo to be put in a coma. He'd have to pay for that, one way or another.

"That enough?" I yelled back to Hammersmith.

"Yeah," Hammersmith shouted back, walking out of the bathroom with the cop. "That's enough."

The cop read both Pete and Ricky their rights, and began walking them outside, where a police car was waiting to take them to the Hall of Justice.

"One favor?" Ricky asked on his way out.

"What?" Hammersmith asked.

"Don't tell Alfredo about the fight?"

"He's gonna find out sooner or later," Hammersmith said.

"Would you tell him then, Sleeper? I don't want to him to read about it in the paper. Tell him I'm sorry."

I nodded. Ricky put his head down and left.

"You crazy bastard," Hammersmith shouted at me. "I don't know how you did it, but you did."

"You think he's telling the truth about not killing Cindy?"

"It doesn't matter. With that testimony, Stezak and Porto are both going down with him. Hard. It doesn't matter if it's for murder or for covering one up. They're done."

"You sure it's enough to get Stezak?"

"More than enough."

"It better be, because my life isn't worth a nickel if it isn't," I said.

"It will be. We'll take Ricky's statement and then I'll take it to Freitas."

"Hold on, I'll walk out with you," I said.

"Where are you going?" Hammersmith asked.

"To the hospital to tell Alfredo."

"Lucky you."

"Could be worse."

"How?" he wondered.

"I could be Alfredo."

59

Saturday, November 11th, 1 a.m.

Hospital visiting hours were over but, like most rules in the Tenderloin, they went ignored.

Alfredo was lying on his side, facing the window. I could see his eyes open in the reflection. "Hi, Sleeper." He must have seen my image in the window. "Where's Ricky?"

I sat down on the edge of his bed. "I think you know."

"They arrested him?"

"Yeah," I said. "You okay?"

"No."

"How did you find out?" I asked.

"Mercedes, that crazy *chica*, returned my necklace to me. The cross was still on it. I knew the one you got from the cop must be his," he said.

"It doesn't make sense to me. Why would Ricky do something like that?"

"He's always been weird about sex. When he was little he'd beat up any girl in the neighborhood who liked him. I thought he was over it. Shit, I thought he was still a virgin."

"For what it's worth, Ricky says the cops set him up. That

it was a cop who killed her."

"Oh yeah?" Alfredo said, perking up.

"Yeah, but even if that's so, I have more bad news I have to tell you."

"Worse than my brother killing a woman?"

"You might think so. It's about the fight." I interpreted his silence as encouragement to continue. "Virgil didn't throw a lucky punch. That cop, Stezak, found out about Ricky and squeezed him for money. A lot of money."

"So?"

"So the cop made Ricky go along with a plan to get the money back. He agreed to fix your fight with Ward."

"Fix my fight? How? I wasn't in on any fix."

"I know you weren't," I said. "Ricky tipped off Pete about how you stand up coming out of your turns."

"He was waiting on me?" he asked.

"Yeah."

Alfredo closed his eyes, the world-shattering truth about his brother seeping inside him. "How could Ricky do that to me?" he asked, facing me.

"Alfredo, there's more. Virgil's gloves had Plaster of Paris in them."

"Plaster of Paris?"

"Cement," I said.

"Did Ricky knew about that, too?"

"No, that was all Pete," I lied. Alfredo had swallowed enough bad news for one night. "He tried to protect you. Why do you think he had you doing all those neck exercises? He didn't want you to get hurt like this."

"He should have told me. I might have taken the fall for him."

"He knew you looked up to him like a father. He didn't want to disappoint you. He couldn't ask you to take this hit for him. Not for what he'd done."

Alfredo turned back toward the window.

"I'm sorry, Alfredo. I'm sorry about it all."

"Could you leave, Sleeper?" he asked. "I want to be alone."

"Yeah," I said. "No problem."

I stopped at the door. I wanted to say something to make it right, but those words didn't exist. They say you don't really know how good a boxer is until he's taken his first punch. Like all boxing wisdom, this was true both in and out of the ring. Alfredo had the unenviable task of recovering from both kinds of punches at the same time.

60

Sunday, November 12th, 5 p.m.

I spent the weekend on Nelson's couch, smoking weed, watching football, and trying to forget about the horrors of the last few months: how the Tenderloin could grind up anyone, even somebody as extraordinary as Alfredo.

I read the Sunday *Chronicle's* article about Ricky's arrest. The fight being thrown was the focus, Cindy's death relegated to a mere footnote. The article was even sparser on details regarding Stezak, noting only that two well-placed San Francisco policemen were implicated. No matter, so long as Stezak and Porto went down soon, I was happy and, more importantly, safe.

"Lori left today for San Mateo," I said to Nelson.

"Why there?"

"She couldn't handle the T.L. anymore, not if she wanted to stay clean. Too many temptations."

"You're cool with that, right?" he asked.

"Yeah. I'm cool with it." San Mateo was a mere twenty miles south, but as far as us maintaining a relationship, it might as well have been Tijuana. I liked to think it was only the T.L. she was escaping and not me. "She has you to thank for her freedom. You paid off her pimp," I said.

"You won the money. Seems like she has you to thank more."

"I know what that record collection meant to you," I said.

"Don't get mushy on me now, Sleeper. It doesn't suit you. I still had enough leftover to buy back a good chunk of them, anyway. So, you moving back into your apartment, now?" he asked.

"Already did."

My phone rang downstairs, but with Lori gone, Nelson sitting across from me, and no yellow Olds circling the block, I ignored it, studying the betting lines instead. *No way the Niners cover against the Rams*, I thought.

"You still think George's murder had to do with Jones?" Nelson asked.

I'd been so caught up in what had transpired the last twenty-four hours that I'd forgotten I'd linked Cindy and George's murders. I saw no reason why Cindy not being killed by the Temple changed anything regarding George. He had still been planning to turn over Prokes's evidence of election fraud, and, thanks to Mazor, the Temple knew it.

"Yeah. I do." I didn't think the identity of Cindy's murderer would change anything with Maguire, either. He wanted a way into the Temple, and "The Letters to Dad" were his ticket.

My phone started ringing again.

"You gonna answer that?" Nelson asked.

I stood up with a moan. I'd lost count of all my injuries: my stabbed leg, my shot lung, my choked neck, and my bitten finger. Ten rings later—persistent bastard, whoever it was—I answered.

"Sleeper. It's Hammersmith. Where you been?"

"At Nelson's. You been calling all morning?"

"We have a problem. You need to leave your apartment."

"Why's that?"

"Ricky killed himself in jail."

"Good," I said.

"Not good," Hammersmith replied.

"Hey, I'm an eye for an eye guy, Hamm—"

"Yeah, I bet Stezak is too."

"Stezak? What the—" Oh. Fuck me. I got it now. Without Ricky they wouldn't be able to prosecute Stezak, placing the bulls-eye squarely on my back again. "You're right, that's a bit of a problem."

61

Sunday, November 12th, 8 p.m.

Since I never told Wethersby I'd left his apartment, I didn't feel the need to inform him I'd returned. I ordered a case of Bud, the fixings for a dozen ham sandwiches, and two bottles of Johnnie from Bell Market, then waited for Hammersmith to stop by after work.

I contemplated leaving San Francisco. New York? Too expensive. L.A.? Too sunny. Boston? Too white. New Orleans? That was a possibility.

Hammersmith knocked on my door at 8 p.m. I'd never invited him to my luxury hideout because I didn't want to subject myself to his ire. Hammersmith viewed himself and Wethersby as mortal enemies. In reality, it was only Hammersmith who saw it that way; I doubted Wethersby spent any time thinking about Hammersmith at all.

"What the hell? Whose place is this?" he asked.

"You don't want to know," I said.

"Not him?" He couldn't even say Wethersby's name.

"Yes, him."

"I'll say this for you, you have range in your friends. Is

that his scotch, too?" he asked.

"He paid for it."

"Then pour me a double."

I poured us both triples and we sat in the small formal living room, the lights of South San Francisco flickering through the windows.

"So what's the plan?" I asked.

"Leave town?"

"I was thinking the same thing," I said. I pulled a cigarette out and offered him one.

"You aren't gonna quit those?"

"You aren't gonna stop asking? I can't believe I have to leave San Francisco. Didn't you guys take down Ricky's statement? Isn't that worth something?"

"Without him in court to corroborate it, it would be worthless."

"So Stezak will continue to terrorize whoever he wants?"

"As long as Moscone is mayor," he said.

"Jesus. I'm beginning to think that blackmail is the only way anything gets done in this city."

"Not the only way, but it wouldn't hurt if you had something on someone."

I lit another cigarette and poured another scotch. "You know what?" I asked. "You aren't so worthless after all, Hammersmith."

"Why's that?"

"Because I might be able to play the blackmail game, too."

62

Wednesday, November 15th, 8:30 p.m.

My plan was a long shot. It required leaps of faith and perfect execution, not two of my strong suits. At least the details could be plotted without my leaving Wethersby's apartment, a prospect I considered no less than a death sentence at this point.

There were many variables, but the plan was dependent upon Tenora's willingness to help. Without her complicity, I could start hitchhiking to the Big Easy right then and there. I wasn't sure when her and Moscone's next rendezvous was scheduled. I hadn't seen them for a few days, so I assumed it wouldn't be long. I was right. Two mornings later, I heard the two of them walk upstairs, separately, as was their custom.

An hour later, I was waiting by my door. As she passed by, always the first to leave, I grabbed her arm and pulled her inside the darkened room. She let out a little gasp, then, recognizing her attacker, offered a look of frustrated resignation.

"Shhhh," I said. She turned to leave. "Don't go. I need to

talk to you. I'm in danger." She studied my face, decided I wasn't lying, and sat down on the couch. We waited in silence until we heard Moscone's footsteps on the stairs. "How's your career training?" I said.

She got up to leave, again. "I thought you were in trouble. I should have known."

"I'm sorry. That was inappropriate."

"But typical for you."

"I'm really in trouble. More trouble than I've ever been in in my life."

"That's saying something."

"A bent cop is trying to kill me," I said.

"A cop? Seriously?"

"Do I look like I'm joking?"

"For once you don't. What happened?"

"You wouldn't believe how it got to this and you probably don't have the time to hear it all. But I need a favor from you. A big favor," I said.

"What?"

"I need you to arrange a meeting for me with the mayor."

"Are you crazy?" she asked.

"Is that a rhetorical question?"

"Why do you need to talk with George?"

"Because I need to convince him to run a sting on this crooked cop."

"I don't know," she sighed.

"This cop is as dirty as they come," I said.

"If he's so dirty, why hasn't he been investigated before?"

"Because he has the goods on everyone, including Moscone."

"George? What goods?"

This was delicate. I wasn't sure how much Tenora knew

about Moscone's sexual proclivities, whether she thought she was special or if she knew she was only another in a litany of young, black mistresses. "Marital infidelity. But not you," I responded quickly to her frightened look. "Way back. Long time ago."

"Oh."

"Tenora, you had to know you're not the first."

"I know. I don't even know what I'm doing with him. He's sweet and fun, but…"

"Isn't that enough?"

She shrugged and shook her head. "No. It isn't. Not for me. How are you planning to convince the mayor if this cop already has dirt on him?"

"The less you know, the better. The one thing I promise is that I'm not dangling you in any part of the deal," I said.

"Let me think about it. I don't want you to mess this up for me. I know I have to break it off with him, but I want it to be on good terms."

"I just need a meeting. Ten minutes."

"Ten minutes?"

"That's it. And I'll be forever in your debt," I said.

"That's not a selling point. I'll think about it and call you later," she said.

"I wouldn't ask if I wasn't desperate."

"I know. I've learned a little about desperation lately, too."

63

Wednesday, November 15th, 3 p.m.

I had a strong feeling Tenora would come through for me. Or maybe I refused to believe otherwise, since there was no other option for me that allowed me to stay in San Francisco.

I had other ducks to align while I waited for her call. I checked in with Donny to see if he was still on board with taking down Stezak about the payoffs. Though he barely had the strength to whisper, I would describe his reply as an emphatic yes. My lone uncertainty about Donny now was whether he would live long enough to carry out the plan.

My next call was to Debbie. I needed to know more about what was in Prokes's notebook. Convinced her phone was tapped by the Temple, she wasn't keen to talk to me for very long. I asked her every detail she could remember about the document in our short conversation. I hung up having a better, if incomplete, understanding of Jones's role in determining the winner of the '75 mayoral election.

Lastly, I called Wethersby. If I was about to blackmail the mayor of San Francisco, I wanted tips from an expert. After circling around the problem for ten minutes, he deduced the essence, as well as the seriousness, of my situation.

"If you're telling me what I think you are, and please don't say anymore, here's what you need to do," he said. "First, you never threaten him. You insinuate, you imply, you suggest. Subtly. But you don't threaten."

"Subtlety is not my forte."

"It needs to be in this conversation. Second, you make him think it's his idea. Lead him to water, he'll drink. Then, flatter him as if you never could have thought of it yourself. I've found that politicians' egos are balloons in need of constant helium."

"Got it. Is that it?"

"Not quite. I'm also giving you the advice I give to lawyers before their first case in court. Practice what you're going to say, out loud. If the first time these words come out of your mouth is when you're talking to him, they'll sound foreign, and odd, like it isn't you talking. You'll stutter, or say the wrong thing, or even worse, sound unconvincing. You can't afford that, especially the unconvincing part."

"Alright."

"Say it out loud. Not to yourself."

"Okay," I said. "Out loud."

"Last thing. When you leave, shake his hand and look him in the eye."

"Why?" I asked.

"Because it's not a deal unless you shake on it."

"What are you guys, twelve years old?"

"I guess we never outgrow some schoolyard conventions," he said.

"If I pull this off, you gonna offer me a job?" I said.

"If you pull this off, you might be offering me one."

The following night, right as I was giving up on Tenora and warming to the idea of the Crescent City, the phone rang.

"Seven a.m. tomorrow," she said.

"Thank you, Tenora."

"Don't thank me. Don't owe me anything. Just don't embarrass me."

"This is my one chance to save my life. I won't blow it. What made you decide to say yes?"

"Partly to see if he'll do something for me."

"And the other part?"

"The other part wants to help you," she said.

"And if he had said no?"

"Then it would have been that much easier to break it off."

"It's a fling," I said. "Don't be too hard on yourself."

"I used to be so sure of myself. Now, I feel...lost."

"Welcome to the club," I said.

"Any advice?"

"Do I seem like I have it all figured out to you?"

We lingered on the phone, listening to each other breathe. "So what are you listening to now?" she asked.

"You know I'm a Teddy Pendergrass guy."

"Oh, I love "Close to You." What about "Only You"?"

"I don't know it," I said.

"Loleatta Holloway? You're slippin', Sleeper."

"I'll check it out," I said.

"You think it says something about us that all we listen to are sad sack breakup songs and neither of us can find our soul mate?" she asked.

"Who said I was looking for one?" I said.

"So, what, I was gonna be a little something on the side?"

"Side, front, back..."

"How about none of the above," she said. "I'll see you tomorrow."

I dismissed her nonsense theory about ballads and lonely hearts, then manically scanned the radio for that Loleatta Holloway song.

64

Friday, November 17th, 6:30 a.m.

I practiced my pitch, out loud, as Wethersby advised. It was good counsel. The first few times I said it, the words sounded like they were coming from someone I abhorred. By the tenth time, they sounded like they were coming from someone I only disapproved of mildly.

Tenora's heels clicked up the stairs at 6:45 a.m. She paused in front of my door for a painstaking fifteens seconds—*keep climbing Tenora*, I silently pleaded—before continuing up the final flight.

A heavier set of footsteps trudged up the stairs at 7:05. At 7:10, I knocked on the door. Tenora answered and ushered me through the empty front living room. I knocked on the cracked bedroom door and stepped inside.

The mayor was sitting at a small desk, legs crossed, hands folded in his lap. "Tenora says you'd like to talk to me about something urgent. Something about corruption in our police force."

"I would," I said.

"Well, then, let's talk," he said.

I emerged from the bedroom thirty minutes later. Tenora was pacing in the living room. I nodded my head and she smiled. The mayor was already on the phone making arrangements with the D.A.

"Thank you," I whispered. "This couldn't have been easy for you."

"Easier than what I'm about to do now," she said, wringing her hands and looking at the bedroom door. I suspected the mayor had had his final roll with Tenora Percy.

Back in Wethersby's apartment, I was on the phone explaining to Hammersmith his role in bringing Stezak to justice. "It has to be you," I said.

"Why?"

"Because I told the mayor you would handle it."

"So I know what I'm getting myself into, what else did you tell the mayor?" he asked.

"I told him I had proof of Jones's illegalities in the last election in Prokes's notes. I added that Tim Stoen was ready to admit to a cover-up in the D.A.'s office. All lies, but believable ones."

"He admitted to it, then?" he asked.

"No. I gave him an out. I said that whether it was true or not, it would make for bad press."

"You bluff a mean hand," Hammersmith said.

"Not really. In the poker game of blackmail, it seems that election fraud trumps adultery," I said.

"He made the right call. Things have changed. Nobody in San Francisco is going to hold adultery against him for long."

"Donny's on board," I continued. "You'll be the one running the sting. Don't screw this up. Make sure Donny is safe."

"It'll take a couple of days to set up. It'll probably go

down on Monday. Lay low for a little while longer and this will all be over soon."

"Thanks, Tom."

"You're welcome, but don't ever, *ever*, call me Tom again."

65

Sunday, November 19ᵗʰ, 8 a.m.

The following morning's headline from *The Chronicle* seared itself into my brain forever:

Rep. Leo Ryan Shot
Ambush at Guyana Airport

My first thought was for Grace and Tim, who had accompanied Congressman Ryan in an attempt to retrieve their son. I scanned the article. The Congressman and four members of the media were shot and probably killed. As many as fifteen others were injured, most of them journalists or part of Ryan's staff. Details were still sketchy as to who the perpetrators were, though there was no doubt in my mind who was behind it. This prompted the disturbing thought that the guns the Temple used might have been bought from Janks.

I turned on the television for an update, only to find *The 700 Club*, *The Big Valley* and *Looney Tunes*. It wasn't until later that night that Van Amburg, the local news anchor, broke in to report on the attack.

By then, the news was worse than what the paper had reported. Much worse. Amburg reported that 400 bodies were found dead in Jonestown as a result of self-inflicted poisoning. Another 500 were missing. They showed aerial views of the camp. It was one mass grave. Bodies were stacked next to and on top of one another. Families were grouped together. Children and babies were in the arms of their parents. They looked like they were sleeping, like it was naptime at the compound. I'd never seen that many dead bodies at once in my life. Not even in photographs of Vietnam. It didn't seem possible.

I knew at least twenty people off the top of my head who'd gone to Jonestown. White friends from the hippie movement who, despite the Temples' call for racial equality, held most of the Temples' prominent posts, and black friends from the Western Addition, who made up the bulk of the congregation. I wondered how many were lying there in the jumble of bodies, four thousand miles away.

I wanted to talk with someone about it, but I couldn't risk leaving the apartment. My first instinct was to call my ex-wife Maggie. She was the one person who made me feel like all was right in the world when it wasn't. She was also the one person who had forbidden me to contact her ever again.

Throughout the rest of the week, the *Chronicle* was front-to-back Jonestown. Each report was grimmer than the last, the death toll creeping higher, the images more and more haunting.

On Tuesday, the paper ran a feature on the Concerned Relatives, who were huddled together under police protection at the Human Freedom Center. There were unconfirmed rumors that Jones had left standing orders with twenty-five assassins in San Francisco to murder any Temple enemies, especially defectors. The rumors were serious enough that the FBI had dispersed fifty agents into the field to track down any leads.

I never received a call from anyone officially scratching the sting on Stezak. They didn't have to. The city was in mourning. For a tragedy that occurred halfway across the world, this one might as well have taken place in Golden Gate Park. Besides, without the threat of Prokes confirming the details of his notebooks, my bluff to Moscone was toothless.

I wondered how quickly the former political coddlers of Jones—Moscone, Brown, Milk, and Caen—would disavow him now. Reports were that Moscone was devastated. He should be. I thought about Cindy and all the other Concerned Relatives who tried to warn everyone about the Temple. I wondered if I could have done more.

The death toll was now over 900 and still rising. The number of people I'd known who were confirmed dead was over thirty. I set a goal to drink a shot of Johnnie and smoke a cigarette for every person I knew who died in Jonestown.

Hammersmith called me after my tenth shot.

"You don't have to tell me. I know the deal is off," I said.

"That isn't why I called. I figured you could piece that together for yourself. I'm calling about Prokes."

"What about him?

"He's alive," Hammersmith said.

"He is?"

"Yeah, he wasn't around to drink the Kool-Aid. He and two other guys were caught trying to sneak out two million dollars in a suitcase. They were gonna give all that money to Russia, the fucking idiots."

"So you think with Prokes alive that Moscone will agree to the deal now?"

"It's worth a shot, isn't it?" he said.

"Maybe," I said.

"What's wrong? You sound out of it."

"Nothing. I'm gonna pass on your offer." I had settled on another plan, a plan that I couldn't relay to Hammersmith. I had put him in some tough ethical spots before, but this one was beyond the pale.

"You leaving town, then?" he asked.

"I have a few things I have to do."

"I'll save you a seat at Donny's."

"Thanks, but that won't be necessary," I said, hanging up.

My new plan was about self-defense. But it was also about revenge. Revenge for George, and for Cindy, and while I was at it, for Alfredo. It was revenge for the 900 people in Guyana as well, whose past due date had been stamped randomly, without sentiment or consequence. I wasn't going to be added that list without a fight, even if it meant putting someone else on it in my place.

At least the guy I had in mind had it coming.

66

Monday, November 27ᵗʰ, 10 a.m.

Donny and I hatched a plan for the following Monday. Time wasn't on either of our sides. Donny more than sympathized with my new course of action, he encouraged it. His exact response was, "I'll die a more peaceful death knowing I outlived that motherfucker."

The plan required no bells and whistles, no fancy two-steps. All it necessitated was me not losing my nerve. Donny would refuse to pay Stezak's protection money and demand a face-to-face meeting with him before the bar opened. I'd be waiting in the bathroom for Stezak to arrive. Then, I'd shoot him.

That was the plan in its entirety. Donny would claim it was a robbery gone bad. If the police didn't believe him, he wasn't worried; he wouldn't live long enough to see the inside of a jail cell anyway.

At nighttime, with the lights dimmed, Donny's bar almost attained a dive bar charm. But in the harsh morning light, it was downright garish, nothing more than a small room with a cement floor, a plywood bar, and a couple of card tables scattered about.

Donny sat by the register behind the bar, wheezing with every breath. "He'll be here in twenty minutes," he managed.

"You sure you're willing to lie for me? If they don't buy your robbery story, it could be tricky. Cop killers aren't long for this world."

"Neither are stage four lung cancer patients. Who knows, it might be the only thing that gets me past St. Peter's gate."

"I think Lara would disagree with that." Lara was Donny's tough as nails daughter who was inheriting the bar.

"You better get in position," he said.

I went to the dingy bathroom opposite the bar and closed the door. I pulled the gun out of my pocket and, for the fifth time that day, checked to make sure it was loaded. Also for the fifth time that day, I checked my conscience to see if it was okay with what was about to go down. Once again, it offered no resistance.

I lit a cigarette. Vowing it to be my last, no matter how the day turned out, I savored every lungful of smoke.

I heard the distinct tap of Stezak's nightstick on the front door. Donny shuffled over and unlocked it. The last detail needed for the plan to work was that Stezak had to be alone. If Porto accompanied him, I wasn't leaving the bathroom.

"Donny, Porto told me we have a problem," Stezak said. He was by himself. There was no going back now. "I told Porto, not from my friend Donny. He's an agreeable guy. But Porto said, maybe the cancer has made him not so agreeable. Who was right, me or Porto?"

"Porto," Donny said.

"Donny, Donny, Donny. Why? Why make trouble now? We've had such a long healthy relationship. And when you're gone, I expect to have the same type of relationship with your daughter. You wouldn't want the two of us to start out on difficult terms when she's in charge, would you?"

"Fuck you," Donny whispered.

"Speak up, Donny. I don't think I heard you right."

It must have taken all the energy Donny could muster to repeat it, but he did, this time as loud as a foghorn in the bay: "Fuck you, Stezak, you piece of shit."

I heard scuffling and opened the bathroom door. Stezak was pulling Donny, all one hundred and twenty pounds of him, over the bar with his one good arm. His other one was still in a sling, a lingering side effect from the cab ride he'd taken with Yuri and me.

"Put him down," I said. Stezak turned his scarred and purple head in disbelief, still holding Donny in the air. I pointed the gun at Stezak's chest. Even I wouldn't miss at this range, no more than ten feet.

He dropped Donny, who fell on top of the bar like a bundle of kindling.

"Sit down, you prick," I said.

"Put the gun away, Sleeper. You're way out of your depth here."

"You're wrong. I've sunk right down to your level," I said.

"Stop with the clever talk. If I'm not out of here soon, Porto will know something is wrong."

"Then I better get this over with."

"Get what over with?"

"Shooting you," I said.

"Be serious, Sleeper. You're no murderer."

"It's not murder if it's self-defense."

"Self-defense? My gun is still in my holster."

"I'm living on borrowed time. We both know that. I'd be dead already if it wasn't for the taxi crashing into a tree."

"Sleeper, I'm sorry I lied to you about that hooker. But that's no reason to do anything you'll regret."

"Who said I'd regret it?"

"You won't be able to live with yourself if you do this. Maybe not right away, but sooner or later it'll eat at you from the inside out."

"You sound like you're talking from first-hand experience," I said.

"You think the T.L. is bad now, you wait until I'm gone. I know everything that goes on here. You watch what happens when some by-the-book pencil pusher runs it. The Tenderloin will swallow him whole and spit him out," he said.

"And the trains ran on time under Mussolini. I've heard it before," I said.

"Damn right they did, you coward," he said, standing up.

"One more question. Who killed Cindy, Ricky or Porto?" With Ricky dead, this was my last chance to know what happened that night.

"Cindy Teague? What, you were in love with her, too? She must have been some great lay."

"Ricky or Porto?" I repeated.

"Neither," he said.

"Come on. Porto has nothing to worry about with Ricky dead. So, who was it?"

"I told you. Neither. Porto went back up to her room and some woman was there, placing the angel on her chest."

"A woman?" I asked.

"Some crazy looking bitch with yellow eyes and gray hair. She fought off Porto and jumped out the window."

287

My disbelief must have shown all over my face.

"You knew her too, huh?" Stezak laughed. "Like I said, you should be called Wrong Way Hayes. Alright, I'm leaving now, Wrong Way. We'll see if you have the balls to finish this."

"This isn't a bluff, Stezak," I said, still stunned by what I'd learned about Cindy's killer.

His chest started heaving, the reality of the situation sinking in. "You won't shoot anybody. You're nothing but a two-bit drunk. A fucking nobody. And you'll always be a nobody."

He stepped toward the door. Donny gave me an imploring look, knowing the dire consequences for both of us if he reached the exit before I shot him.

Stezak turned and went for his gun. I think. At least that's what I tell myself. Whatever movement he may or may not have made, I pulled the trigger first. He stopped walking. I pulled it again, and again, the bullets decorating his chest like buttons sewed on a double-breasted suit by a blind tailor.

Stezak fell against the bar, gasping for air. He tried to steady himself on a stool, but it collapsed under his weight, taking Stezak down with it. Blood spilled over the front of the bar and dripped onto his forehead, his lifeless arms unable to wipe it away.

"Give me the gun," Donny said.

I heard Porto slam his car door shut.

"Why?"

"Give it to me." Donny said.

"No," I said. "I can't let you take the rap for me."

"Don't be stupid, Sleeper. This will close the book on

288

this forever. I'm never gonna see the inside of a jail cell. We both know that."

Porto pounded on the door.

"But—"

"Don't make me put you on our list, Sleeper. 'People who go to jail for no reason.' Just promise me you'll look after Lara."

I stared at him, dumbstruck.

"Give me the fucking gun!" Donny yelled.

I handed it to him.

"Now out the back way," he said.

Porto was wailing on the door now, the hinges splitting open.

"We're good?" I asked Donny.

"Never better," he said. "Now, go!"

I sprinted out the back door at the same time as the front crashed open. Ten steps down the alley, I heard another gunshot.

I whirled around and ran back toward Donny's. If Porto had shot Donny, I was going to make today a daily double. As I approached the door, I realized what had happened. Porto hadn't shot Donny, nor vice versa. Donny had taken himself out of his pain for good.

I dashed down the alley to Taylor Street and hung a right on Turk. I heard a police siren already approaching from the east. Then another. I saw lights coming south on Jones. How could the cops be here so fast? I stopped and faced away from the street, putting my hands over my head. The cars, now totaling four police and two ambulance, went racing by, uninterested in me whatsoever.

I watched the cars head west on Turk toward City Hall,

some other crime taking precedence over the one I'd committed at Donny D's. Judging by the number of police cars wailing, it was taking considerable precedence.

A woman in a green Pinto passed slowly and rolled down her window. She shouted something inaudible to me.

"What?" I asked, stepping toward the curb.

"Mayor Moscone's been shot. He's dead," she cried, and continued down Turk, yelling her information to every pedestrian along the way.

The sirens blew louder. If not already engulfed in chaos, San Francisco sounded like it was on the precipice of it. I was comfortable with this fact. More comfortable than I ever thought I would be.

1979

EPILOGUE

Saturday, March 24th, 9 p.m.

Alfredo stood in the middle of the ring with his hand raised over his head by the referee. Alfredo was smiling like nothing had happened. Like he'd never been in a coma. Like his brother hadn't almost killed him. Like he was still going to be the next Roberto Duran.

Except it was different. He'd beaten a nobody in his return bout by unanimous decision. A year ago, the fight wouldn't have lasted three rounds. It could have been rust. It could be I was being too hard on him. We'd find out soon enough, but Billy agreed with me. He thought it was physical, that Alfredo had lost a few tenths of a second off his punches. I thought it was mental, that Alfredo, no matter how hard he tried to mask it, now had that shred of doubt that the rest of us possess.

Hammersmith read my body language. "Hey, at least he's fighting again," he said.

"Yeah."

"It's not enough for you, though, is it?"

"No."

293

"That's your problem, you know that?" Hammersmith said.

"What's that?"

"Nothing is ever good enough for you."

Hammersmith was only partly right. For the bulk of us, good was good enough. Like for Lori, who was still clean in San Mateo, waitressing at a diner. Or for Tenora, who'd already been offered a job at Wethersby's firm after graduation. Even for Hammersmith, who'd found a woman he liked spending time with more than any bar.

Good was also good enough for me. I suffered an occasional bad night's sleep over Stezak's death, but that was the extent of my remorse. On the nights my conscience weighed me down, I was comforted by a deeper, undeniable truth: that the world was a better place without Stezak. As for criminal repercussions, there were none. His murder, having occurred on the same day and approximate time as the Moscone and Milk assassinations, barely registered, especially since Donny had wrapped it up so perfectly.

Good would have been good enough for Maguire, who, unable to work his way into the Temple in time to stop the massacre, would carry that failure around with him the rest of his life.

Of course good was out of the question for the Concerned Relatives, none of whom ever saw their loved ones alive again.

But good wasn't good enough for Alfredo. Alfredo's gift deserved to be fully realized like the other greats who'd come before him, but who'd also been given the good fortune of time to fulfill their potential.

"Maybe the rest of the world should be a little more demanding," I said.

"Why, so everyone can be a miserable bastard like you? You should try being happy like the rest of us," he said.

Happiness, I thought. *Should we add that one to our list, too, Donny?*

AUTHOR'S NOTE

Historical Fiction is an elastic, messy genre, where real people and events collide with imaginary characters and plotlines. It can be many things, but one thing it is not is actual history. The fiction writer is obligated to conform to facts as much as the historian is bound by the rules of Shakespearean tragedy.

For *Tenderloin*, my guiding principle was not to offer a revised version of history, but to construct a story based on historical events that was plausible, and nothing more. I tried to only introduce facts about Mayor Moscone, Jim Jones and the Peoples Temple, or any other historical figures that were reported contemporaneously to the events in the book.

The *Chronicle* or *Examiner* reported the Temples' gun running and Jim Jones's mob ties prior to the mass murder at Jonestown. Also widely reported was The Concerned Relatives' fear of retribution. The monitoring, bullying, and intimidation of Temple opponents were thoroughly documented, as was the existence of Temple security, The

Angels, the mysterious woman in charge, and the murder of Bob Houston, who was found on the railroad tracks on October 5th, 1976, the day of his defection from the Peoples Temple.

While evidence of voter fraud committed by the Temple was eventually confirmed, there is no evidence that Mayor Moscone knew about the fraud at the time. However, Michael Prokes and Jim Jones *did* meet with Moscone before the election; the election *was* decided by fewer than 5,000 votes; Jim Jones *was* named Chair of the San Francisco Housing Commission after the election; and Tim Stoen, still a member of the Temple at the time, *was* placed in charge of the voter fraud investigation in the D.A.'s office. These historical facts allowed me to plausibly build the voter fraud storyline.

There is no evidence that Michael Prokes was planning to betray Jim Jones. That part of the plot was entirely invented. In fact, on March 13, 1979, Prokes called a press conference at a Modesto hotel, read a statement defending Jonestown, retreated to the hotel bathroom, and blew his brains out with a revolver.

An indispensable resource for the Jim Jones plot was *The Raven*, by Tim Reitterman, an *Examiner* reporter who was injured in the shootout that took Congressman Leo Ryan's and four others' lives. *The Raven* is a must read for anyone interested in the history of the Temple and the tragedy at Jonestown.

Mayor Moscone's sexual infidelities and preferences were known within a wide circle of people at the time, and documented in the excellent book on the Moscone-Milk murders, *Double Play*, by Mike Weiss. Moscone's dalliance with Tenora was inspired by a relationship detailed by Weiss between Moscone and a Western Addition community activist. Like *The Raven*, anyone interested in the Dan White murders should start their reading with Weiss's account.

The "Letters to Dad" were found in Jonestown and reproduced verbatim.

Joe Mazor, while not betraying the Concerned Relatives in the manner depicted in the book, did receive money from the Temple for privileged information about the Concerned Relatives, in particular Grace and Tim Stoen. The eye patch was factual, as well.

Newman's Gym was a Tenderloin fixture for over fifty years, as was Billy Newman. Apart from the gym's location, its history, and Billy's widely known generosity of spirit, nothing about the Alfredo Flores storyline is based on any actual people or events.

Finally, on February 26, 1980, shortly after publishing *Six Years with God*, an account of their years in the Temple, Jeannie and Al Mills, as well as their daughter Daphene, were murdered in their Berkeley home.

Their killer or killers have never been apprehended.

CPSIA information can be obtained
at www.ICGtesting.com
Printed in the USA
LVOW10s0327050517

533330LV00001B/76/P